SIMON PETRIE

CONSIDERATION
OF THE METHOD OF DISPOSAL

First published in Australia in 2026

Please direct all enquiries to the publisher at:
fomalhaut451@gmail.com

ISBN 978-0-6483837-1-0

Typeset in Adobe Garamond Pro / Candara
Cover illustration by James Morrison

National Library of Australia Cataloguing-in-Publication entry

Title:	Consideration of the Method of Disposal / Simon Petrie.
ISBN:	9780648383710 (pbk.)
Subjects:	Science fiction, Australian.
Other Authors / Contributors:	
	Morrison, James, editor.
	Morrison, James, cover art.
Dewey Number:	A823.4

SIMON PETRIE

CONSIDERATION
OF THE METHOD OF DISPOSAL

ALSO BY SIMON PETRIE

(GUERLINE SCARFE MURDER MYSTERIES)

Matters Arising from the Identification of the Body

Reappraisal of the Circumstances Resulting in Death

(OTHER FICTION SET ON TITAN)

Wide Brown Land

Soft Dim Skies

(OTHER FICTION INEXPLICABLY NOT SET ON TITAN)

Flight 404

Murder on the Zenith Express: the Gordon Mamon collection

80,000 Totally Secure Passwords That No Hacker Would Ever Guess

Tremendously Inconveniencing A Great Many Photons

The 1001 Top Immortality Treatments You Must Try Before You Die

Wayfaring Stranger

I Have No Legs And I Must Manspread

PROLOGUE

The child was the worst. For years afterward that young boy tormented her, with the way it had happened, with what they'd done to him. With the adults it was still bad, but those at least had understood the risks of failure, even the risks borne by full success; they'd understood, or they should have. A boy that age—or this boy, at least—was oblivious of the subtext; what the grown-ups told him was just how it was, that was plain whenever she'd had cause to talk with him, to provide him with words of comfort in the face of his mother's slow deterioration, and then the more rapid turn which had forced them to act with speed, if not with haste. They'd tried, both herself and Ilhan, to convey to the child that he would need to say farewell to his mother soon, if only for a short time. The mother had sought, too, to help with this, during her more lucid intervals. He'd see her again, she told him, though she couldn't tell when; he would just need to wait. But he'd been so distraught, across the hours during which they had been preparing to put his mother under, had pleaded not to be left behind; they'd refused, of course, it wasn't appropriate, a child like that, they'd received no guidance covering such cases, in a metabolic sense, quite aside from the ethical aspects; and his father would be back for him, if not days then weeks at most, they would look after him until then. Then with the mother already in process—they'd had to, any delay would be exposing her to more risk—they'd explained this to the boy, too, as best they could, *this is the time we were telling you about earlier,* speaking with patience and with as much understanding as they could show him; then they'd heard about his father's death, and Fish had said it might actually be for the best if the boy went under too, the family had been quite clear when the waivers were being filled out, that they didn't want the next of kin involved, and she never knew the reason for that, and she didn't think Fish did either, though obviously it was too late to wonder that now. They could work it on bodyweight, Fish explained, getting caught up in the technicalities; bodyweight, there was nothing magical about that, metabolism was metabolism; and it would mean the boy and the mother had each other, at least, immediately familiar and recognisable to each other, when they brought her back, after however long that might be. It still felt wrong, it still was wrong, which was why it felt so; but Fish was in charge; Fish took responsibility. It was his signature, after all, on all of the authorisation.

So they put the boy under, shortly after the mother: induced coma, then progressively larger dosages of the protectant, before the final step in the process. It had been peaceful, the kid had confidence in them.

Two days had passed, and there were always things to do, even if it was quieter now with their charges all having been processed. The next morning, Fish had called her and the other two medics together, a staff meeting in his cramped and too-warm office. She'd looked at Vaara, and then at Ilhan; he'd returned her quizzical glance, she didn't lift her gaze at all. They were standing; their supervisor remained seated. Then Fish had spoken, in a shaken voice, a voice drained of all its habitual command.

You need to do me now, he'd told them. Just an hour between each dose, that'll be sufficient, that'll have to be sufficient. He coughed, more a rattle than a full paroxysm; nonetheless it took longer than it should have for him to regain control of his breathing. He added: There isn't time to take it slower.

She was affronted, refused, glancing again to Vaara and Ilhan for support. Surely Fish could see that they couldn't.

Fish couldn't see that. He stood, and she winced to see what that slight action, in Titan's gentle gravitational field, had cost him; he was sweating, shaking. Do you think I set this up out of altruism? he snarled at them, finding some reserves of steel somewhere. And she noticed—now that she forced herself to heed his appearance, to see past the garb—how gaunt he was, how lacking in the muscle tone he'd carried even one week ago, how blatant the pain that showed despite all the meds that were meant to mask it. How old he'd become, how pallid, a deterioration faster even than had been the boy's mother. Fish was right; he'd be gone soon, they needed to put him under. He prepped them, all the while in a growing agony as he briefed them and tested them on the parts of the process with which they were not already practiced.

As they'd put him under—and it had not been peaceful, he had resisted at the last, as though in premonition—she realised that all Fish's signatures on all the forms were void, for where, now, was Fish? It was her who was in charge now. She'd never wanted that, did not welcome it now.

They did the tests, unconscionably delayed, two weeks later, or was it three? And as she and Ilhan pored over the test results, looking for some explanation, some loophole in what they were seeing, it slowly became horribly clear that they wouldn't be bringing anyone back, ever.

They'd taken a further couple of days to do what needed to be done: she'd worked out how to clear the facility, to erase the traces of what had happened here, and who it had happened to; Ilhan had managed to access the facility's funds, and had untraceably forwarded for each of them a sum which she claimed to be an equal share, which frankly was doubtful in the circumstances, it seemed too low, but nobody had had the spirit to challenge it. They'd all parted ways, the medics and the support workers, both literally and metaphorically.

One by one, the others had gone over the years. She received news of Ilhan's way four years later: overdose, in some small arcology she'd never heard of. With Habibi also it had been substance abuse, a decade or so later; Vaara had been heart failure, twelve years or so after that. Studholme, the oldest of any of them, had lasted longer than the others; old age had claimed him perhaps fifteen years ago.

Her way was less personally destructive than Ilhan's or Habibi's: she had remade herself, to the extent possible, with a plausible employment history just sufficiently edited from truth; then she had found someone who could fix it, could tie up the last loose end for her. With each of the others who died in the following years, it felt as though her life received a fresh start. She could outlive her problems.

But there was still the boy; he'd haunted her, for years afterward. What they'd done to him.

ONE

Fil wasn't hurt in the crash, not really: the T-suit had readied itself in the half-dozen seconds she was airborne before she hit and slid to an ungainly halt. The hastily redistributed insulation had shielded her, in large part, from any sense of impact; her suit hadn't cracked; she'd sustained nothing worse than some probable bruising on her thigh and forearm. No, the problem was her bike's front skid, shorn off just forward of the stem by the obstruction in the iceway. It meant they had no prospect of getting back to Hunten before nightfall.

Or rather, as he explained to her, it meant *she* had no such prospect, for his own skidbike was still unblemished. He'd had time to swerve, and then to brake. But he couldn't brook delay, with five hundred klicks still to cover and with his next series of shifts due to start in just fifteen hours. It made sense for him to press ahead; and his bike was a racer, no pillion; no passengers. But she had power to spare aboard both the bike and the suit, and ample oxygen purification capacity in the latter; and they were close enough, here, to the main Kuiper-Hunten thoroughfare that she could walk, in just one hour, or two max, to a point where there would be plenty of long-haul traffic which could stop to assist her. Or if she preferred simply to wait with the bike, he'd make a report, when he was underway and close enough to Hunten's comms towers for reception, so the rescue services would know where to find her. He was so close to a result; she understood, didn't she, that his work was important to him?

Yes, she certainly understood. She'd learnt that much about him, in abundance, these past few days. She didn't voice what she thought he didn't understand; and she was glad, as she watched the aft lights of his Hainan Speedster fade in the distance ahead, that she'd ignored his several suggestions in a certain direction, hadn't let things go too far in that rented room in Owen.

They'd been following an unmarked trail for the past several hours, a trail he'd known of somehow, certainly not a major route but not virgin Titanian terrain either; the iceway had clearly seen use, perhaps by transport vehicles, construction vehicles, prospectors maybe, looking to cut a little time on getting between Hunten and Owen, or to connect to the so-called midland route leading to the distant southern settlements of Strobel and Hevelius. It was, in truth, a more rugged trail than she'd expected, and surely rougher than he'd expected also, but she'd thought her bike would go alright, probably better than his. It had been one of the reasons she'd taken the lead, so he could be alerted to any hazards which might challenge the Speedster. It had worked out that way, sure, but her bike was inoperable. And he'd ridden off, so as not to be late for work, for a gig with, really, no particular time pressures or due dates—as he'd told her, himself, not two hours ago, as though it were a selling point in his favour, as though there were any such. He'd ridden off, leaving her stranded several hundred klicks from the nearest active settlement. She understood, didn't she?

She understood.

She switched her comms channel, so he wouldn't be able to call back.

The skidbike was a Xu Powerglide, nearly new; it was Fil's most valuable possession. Fifty kilowatts, a range of two thousand seven hundred kilometres, a top speed of eighty-five klicks a standard hour: not that she'd ever ridden it that fast, but it was good to know the option was there. Or rather, it had been good, and it had been there. With the skid shorn off, it wasn't.

The sensible thing: leave the bike, walk to the trade route. Catch a ride to Hunten. Or to Kuiper, if that was all that was on offer. Return for the bike sometime in the next several days, once she'd had a replacement front skid assembly printed.

She wouldn't do that. It was a Xu Powerglide, almost completely hers now, and she couldn't simply leave it out in the open like this. She'd wait, he'd send a report, a rescue team would arrive maybe ten, maybe twenty hours from now. Surely he'd contact the authorities, surely he wasn't so self-obsessed that he'd neglect the requirement to do so, nobody on Titan could be so negligent. They'd find her here, guided by her suit's carrier wave or by the bike's emergency beacon, once she'd figured out how to activate the latter. It'd be darker by then, whenever they reached her, but she'd never feared the darkness. It was necessary just to wait, and she could do that. She had stamina, her suit had media; she'd be fine. Not that that in any sense excused him, riding off like that and leaving her here.

The shadows lengthened, the light diminished, brown fading unhurriedly toward black. There was still a smudge, you wouldn't call it a glow, merely some grainy parody of beige on the western horizon, where the sun's rays were struggling to shine up the upper atmosphere. That smudge would spread as it ebbed, would ensure there was some dim diffuse light throughout the night, centred near the western edge, but it'd get darker than she'd been used to as a child; not the Saturn-lit gloaming which had held nocturnal sway in Trafton, where she'd grown up. Out here, several hundred klicks west of Hunten, it was too far farside here for ring-shine, but that didn't bother her. No stars visible through the upper-atmospheric haze, no lights signifying civilisation anywhere to the horizon, no problem. Just her, her broken skidbike, and the slow-fading light. The noises of her suit's processes, the noises of herself within the suit—breathing, air circulation, the redistribution of fluid within the suit's insulating layers—and perhaps beneath that, the sough of the low insistent breeze that she could feel trying to find a weak point, any weak point, among the reinforced and servoed joints of her well-insulated T-suit.

Perhaps, nonetheless, it might be pragmatic to retrace her journey on foot, back to the point of impact, to reclaim the bike's broken skid and to see just what obstacle had caused it to shear off. She'd need detail such as that to lodge an insurance claim for repair, and it was all best done while there was still enough shine left to the sky, so she could find her way back to the body of the bike once she'd retrieved the front skid.

She oriented herself, started walking. It was further back, along the shadow-pocked umber ice of the makeshift track, than she'd thought it would be, a good fifty metres, not a great distance but long enough when one is searching for an object in failing light. Partway there, through a gap between the dark ice ridges off to her left—to the southeast—she could see a structure, single-storey and clearly derelict, some distance away. It wasn't marked on the trailway map, which likely meant it had been deserted a good many years. Such structures always awoke mixed feelings in her: it was interesting to explore them, certainly, and she'd been willing enough to check out with him the hab they'd stopped at the previous day, before they'd reached Owen, but there was a heightened sense of loss about such places too: someone or some group of people had made the effort, and it was never a small effort, to make a space within which to prevail against the Titanian environment, but had lost the struggle.

The ice changed character as she neared the protrusion; it slickened, lost granularity, shone up so annoyingly in her suit's headlamps that she bade them switch off. Her T-suit's bootsoles slipped, responded with enhanced grip; her servoes pushed back to arrest a stumble. The unexpected reaction unsettled her.

She found the obstacle she must've hit, blocky and surprisingly obtrusive. She couldn't make out its nature in the fading illumination, so she called up the headlamps again, narrow beam. Two cones of intrusive white light against the surrounding gloom.

She'd never been afraid of the darkness, but perhaps that had been a mistake, because when she saw, in the failing light, what it was that her bike had impacted on—what the severed front third of the Xu's front skid was still embedded in—she started to scream and did not know how to stop.

TWO

Kalinda's office had changed in the past year. A larger desk, less guest seating, no more floor-to-ceiling aquarium which had once been the room's focal point, its former position marked out against the wall and floor only by a shape in imperfectly tone-matched tiles. Guerline wondered off-handedly what had happened to the aquarium, and more particularly to its occupants, those little living liquid blobs of quick colour and indecision. Without the fishtank, the room felt colder; or maybe it was that Kalinda's thermal preference had shifted.

Kalinda had changed in other ways too: not just greyer but stockier, yet somehow taller too. Lifts maybe. Still the monobrow, still the predilection for purple linen. Unreasonably tidy desk.

Guerline Scarfe's former supervisor took her seat; after a few seconds, wondering whether or when there was going to be an explanation for why she'd been called in to her old place of employment, Guerline took her own. Soft seat, yielding too much.

'The thing is,' Kalinda began, as though she was merely continuing a year-delayed conversation, 'we may have something here for you. If the terms were agreeable to you.'

'What would the terms be?' Guerline asked.

It was, it turned out, not the question Kalinda wished to answer, or at any rate it was not the question she did answer, to begin with. 'Harini's off, as of next week, Stefan off the week after, both of them for a standard year at least—maternity—and Rayah is currently off sick, has been for the past two weeks and we cannot be sure when she'll be back.'

'You want me to run investigations,' said Guerline, trying to work out whether she felt insulted or flattered. 'You're short-staffed, and you want me to run investigations so the work doesn't build up.'

'We've got the staff for that,' replied Kalinda. 'It's tight, but it's manageable, insh'Allah. What we don't have is the staff to audit the completed cases.'

Insulted emerged victorious. 'You want me to perform cleanup on closed cases?' Guerline asked, striving to lean forward against the too-soft seat. 'Case cleanup, just to cover your shortfall until Rayah gets back—'

'No,' Kalinda said, and did that thing with her palms, the 'calm-down' gesture that seldom worked as intended, at least not with Guerline. 'I mean yes, cleanup, if you wish to call it that, but we both know there's a definite skill to auditing, and you have those skills, however little it sometimes seemed that you liked applying them. This would be ongoing. A way back. Into the Department, into something not too functionally distinct from what you had before. If you can keep your head down.'

'My head down?'

'You displayed a certain… adventurism with the Hainan/Morgenstein follow-up. I shouldn't need to tell you… we can't have that. Head down, nose clean, no going off-script. If something comes up that goes against that—and it really shouldn't, not with the last several months' closures— you report it as appropriate, leave it for others to follow through. Colleagues with more judgment than to go in tilting at windmills. Are you in?'

'Auditing.' She didn't mean to place that tone on it, but it snuck in. Maybe in response to the sense that Kalinda was goading her. Guerline guessed that the Hainan/Morgenstein outcome, with the accusations she'd levelled against a wealthy and well-connected businessman—accusations fully supported by the horrific details which she had uncovered—had perhaps caused deeper problems for the Department than she had appreciated.

Was she being offered a role here, or was her former supervisor seeking to settle a score?

'Think of it as a probationary phase,' Kalinda suggested. 'Of, I must admit, somewhat variable duration. But we will, in due course, need your skills as an investigator. If.'

'How long would I have to decide?'

'Things are tight. An answer now would be appreciated.'

She knows I don't have anything else. Held her pause for as long as she dared, for the sake of dignity or independence or some such. 'Alright then,' she replied, her eyes finding their way back to the absent aquarium.

'Welcome back, Guerline.'

She managed two years without incident. Two years head down, two years nose clean, two years on-script. Two years in which Nikita grew two years older, which should not have surprised her, yet somehow it caught her unawares: two years more solid, two years more sullen, two years less remaining of his childhood. Nearly twelve now, and another syllable dropped: now he preferred to be known simply as 'Nik', would no longer respond to 'Niki', considered it too childish. It was one of hundreds of small shifts in her son's character, markers of the tectonic movements which would be wrought during the seismically active years of adolescence. There was still a connection, a mother-child interaction there, but it had changed and, Guerline knew, would need to change further. Some days she did not understand him at all; at such times, largely, she let him be. Each alternate week, she delivered him back to his father; each alternate week, she wondered which version of her son she'd be seeing when he came back to her.

There was work also, which on the whole was a positive thing. Two years. The work was often dull, routine—people's problems had a tendency to replicate the trials of others to a greater or lesser extent—but completing a task was rewarding nevertheless. After several months, Kalinda had placed Guerline once again in charge of some of the department's active investigations: Stefan would not be returning from leave, Donna and Sintra had both left, Rayah had moved to a reduced workload to assist with management of her ongoing health issues. Guerline couldn't help wondering whether, had that combination of personnel changes not occurred, she might have been kept on indefinitely at the uninspiring if necessary task of closed-case auditing; she knew that Kalinda would find some mechanism to evade the question if asked directly. Kalinda herself was, in any event, gone soon after: headhunted by the equivalent agency in Hunten, three thousand kilometres westward across the stained-ice plains of northern Xanadu. The new supervisor, Toan, was a difficult woman to warm to; or perhaps it was merely that Kalinda had briefed the new starter forcefully on the need to keep several of the investigators, Guerline in particular, on a short rein. Head down, nose clean. Guerline kept at it, sought to work around Toan's insistence on adherence to metrics and to a protocol which didn't always fit the situation, yet sought also always to ensure that her supervisor was fully briefed as to why the protocol should be adjusted in particular circumstances; and slowly, she thought, she earned Toan's trust, her respect. On-script. A balancing act. She was gradually assigned more difficult cases, dealt with them with tidy professionalism. The strictures placed on her relaxed, bit by bit. Two years became two and a half. Two and three quarters.

Then she was assigned the task of Filomene Bayley, and it was clear almost immediately there'd be problems.

THREE

It was, ironically enough, through Kalinda's intercession that the matter of Fil Bayley was assigned to Guerline. Whether this was due to any prior acquaintance, on her former supervisor's part, with the Bayley-Petrakis-Othman family, or whether it was merely a recommendation resulting from Kalinda's surely brief interaction with Fil's case, as the supervisor of the Hunten caseworker assigned to the task of resolving the young woman's sudden onset of trauma, Guerline couldn't establish. Certainly she didn't see herself as the best investigator to deal with the situation: within the department, Monifa was widely recognised as having a special sensitivity in addressing the requirements of cases involving sexual abuse or assault, a circumstance strongly suggested by the nonetheless incompletely recorded particulars of Fil Bayley's situation.

The known facts were these. Bayley, a junior geochem analyst at Hunten Refined Minerals, had declared herself unfit for work following an extended break. Counselling had been initiated, by the young woman, but had been abandoned after one and a half notably unproductive sessions; Fil had decamped to her family home, back in Trafton. There was something about the settlement of Owen, a skidbike, abandonment by a male companion—whether boyfriend or mere acquaintance wasn't clear—and two nights spent in the cab of an ore hauler with a taciturn older woman who, from the sound of it, had exceeded the hauler's recommended maximum speed to deliver her hitchhiker to Hunten in time for the latter's work shift, a return-to-work opportunity which Fil had waived. It wasn't much to go on. Something had happened on the skidbike excursion, that was evident.

The 'family home'—her mother's quarters and her maternal grandparents' residence—constituted two not-quite-adjacent properties on the Aqua Level of corridor 7, a desirable enough location with good access to Trafton's sole expanse of manicured parkland. It was closer to Scarfe's own home than to the department, so Guerline paid a visit as her workday ended. The door she tried was, it transpired, the grandparents'; the woman who came to the entrance, who answered to the name of Liv Petrakis, was a cheery slim-boned woman in a floral-patterned housecoat. Yes, her granddaughter was at her daughter's abode, two doors down.

Sandalwood, patchouli, vanilla: one of those fragrances intended to evoke calm, Guerline wasn't sure which, she wasn't good with scent other than as a marker of air quality. But a heavy aroma, regardless, overly sharp, aggressively cloying. She had to refocus to explain to (she presumed) Fil's mother her purpose in visiting. Guerline Scarfe. With the department. It was important to understand, and to know how best to societally address, any significant aspects of difficulty, or loss, or trauma which any citizen of Trafton had undergone. Fil could participate as much, or as little, as she wished. If she was in, if this time suited.

Paschel Othman was a dark-complexioned middle-aged woman of medium height, her eyes concealed behind a wraparound workscreen. She made no response for several seconds following Guerline's introductory remarks, turned her head away briefly before she spoke. 'She's been through this. In Hunten.'

'I appreciate that,' replied Guerline, making a conscious effort to not be irked by the other's distracted drawl. 'Nonetheless, if Filomene is willing to talk, I'm ready to listen.'

'I'll check.' There was no invitation into the living quarters, so Scarfe waited at the door. Sometimes there was a lot of that. From several doors further down Corridor Seven, a briefly open doorway made audible a domestic argument in full flourish, something about the need to keep the noise down while the child slept. Sometimes there was a lot of that too.

After several minutes, Othman's daughter approached to meet Guerline. Fil Bayley was tall, well-proportioned, with an athletic physique and what Guerline suspected were the fading remnants of a solarium tan. 'You asked to see me,' Bayley explained, a personification of enthusiasm's absence.

'Yes. This might work best if we sit down and talk.'

'Here?'

'If that's comfortable for you, yes.'

Paschel, Fil's mother, was using the lounge for what seemed to be some kind of remote tutorial activity, so Fil led Guerline through to the dining room. Moulded polymer seating around a square C-fibre table. Guerline took her seat first; the other opted for an adjacent seat, rather than the one opposite. Closer but less amenable to eye contact.

'First off,' said Guerline, 'these are the rules I must follow. You're invited to speak freely. Any notes I make from our conversation must meet your agreement for inclusion in your file, excepting only information relating to the commission of a crime or information the exclusion of which could place another's life or health in danger; details in the latter categories must be made available to the relevant authorities. The file's contents remain accessible to you, to myself during the active life of your case, and to my supervisor should certain thresholds of concern be met; the file will be retained for five standard years, during which time a deidentified summary of any relevant findings will be made by the department; after five standard years have elapsed, the file will be destroyed, with indefinite retention only of the deidentified summary, the text of which will be shared with you to ensure full transparency. Should all relevant parties agree—by which I mean you, myself, my supervisor should certain thresholds be met, any agencies or authorities previously notified in response to specific sensitive circumstances concerning the life or health of yourself or another person—your information within the file can be deleted sooner than the five-standard-year upper limit, on an agreed timescale; this is true also of the deidentified summary. That's a mouthful, I know; it's broadly similar to the guidance Hunten would have followed; and by way of disclosure, I have been given a summary of the information you shared with my Hunten counterpart, though that information is retained only by Hunten and has not been placed in your file here, which is currently empty. You may disengage with the process at any point, with no obligation to re-engage, though such re-engagement will remain available should you wish it for a period of one hundred and twenty standard days. Should the case have an interpersonal basis involving another party within this jurisdiction, your own disengagement will not pause my consultations with other relevant parties unless the department is fully satisfied that there is no societal risk accompanying cessation. Are you in agreement with the stated conditions of our interaction?'

There was a facial expression, a shrug. Fil's eyes briefly met Guerline's.

'I'll need a verbal response, I'm afraid,' said Guerline.

'Okay.'

'Excellent. Then let's start. Anywhere you like.'

'Anywhere I like?' Fil's intonation, her mildly alarmed expression, made it sound like a perceived threat.

'Yes. For example, tell me about your life here in Trafton.' *We can get to the more difficult stuff later.*

Her first consultation with Fil Bayley was in some measure inconsequential: nothing of real note was disclosed, merely some details of childhood, upbringing, schooling, vocational training. Queried as to the situation of her father, Fil replied that she'd never had one, except in the purely biological sense: her mother had contracted for pregnancy by an unidentified donor, and had raised her daughter with the grandparents' assistance. It was a point of difference for Bayley's upbringing, but a minor one as such things went, and the young woman seemed willing to discuss it with equanimity, if also with the hesitancy with which she tended to approach her release of any other utterance within that first meeting with Guerline. So, not a groundbreaking discussion but a foundational one nonetheless; Guerline sensed that it would be best not to rush the case's disclosure of anything regarding the problematic incident or incidents which had led to Bayley's self-imposed isolationism. She resolved to probe gently at the second consultation, scheduled for the following week.

That second meeting, at the grandparents' residence while Liv Petrakis and her husband attended a live music performance in Trafton's cultural precinct, was similarly low-key. Guerline was led to an upper-level room dominated, in the far corner, by the scaffold, weights and resistive springs of a static X-rig—'Not mine,' the young woman explained, 'that's my grandfather's, I'd be in trouble if I used it'—but clearly, Guerline mused, Fil must follow some sort of exercise regime, such muscle tone wasn't typical of settlement dwellers. In any event, the dialogue was smoother this time; Fil was more voluble, less guarded, which might have indicated a greater measure of acceptance of Scarfe's role or might equally have resulted from the difference in venue, imprecations against unsanctioned X-rig use notwithstanding. It was a positive marker either way, and Guerline was content to allow Fil to find her own path into the problematic discussion which would follow, in good time, at a future time as it transpired.

That future time was a further week ahead, back in the Othman residence, behind a closed door through which Paschel Othman's parallel, workscreen-mediated discussion with her students occasionally made itself audible. The conversation with Fil took a different direction than that which the investigator had anticipated; and it gave Guerline a problem. It might not be possible to manage the rest of the case at a pace with which Fil would remain comfortable.

She ensured Toan was briefed before she took the next step. She thought of Kalinda as she did so, wondering whether this was the reason her former supervisor had recommended that Guerline be the investigator to take Fil Bayley's case. Monifa might have the most sensitive skills in cases involving sexual assault or abuse, or domestic violence; Rayah was excellent in handling deep-seated questions of personal identity; but nobody could touch Guerline Scarfe on grief.

On the second attempt, the call went through, was accepted audio-only. Guerline announced herself, seeking audibility against what sounded like, and very likely was, a toddler in full meltdown against the world's manifold injustices.

'I'll call you back,' she was told; and after ten minutes, the call came. Full AV. Prabha Braun looked weary, harried, which spiked a sense of guilt in Guerline. She'd clearly contacted the officer off-shift; she could have chosen instead another point of contact, a more official channel into Hunten pol, rather than this one person with whom she had some previous brief acquaintance.

It would have been better, perhaps, if her history with Braun had been a more nuanced thing, deeper, more faceted. Had that been the case, there'd be a solid reason to arrange a meeting, whether face-to-face or remote. There'd be aspects of connection: Guerline could have asked how parenthood was going, could have asked how the woman was adjusting to life and work in a different settlement. She could have eased into the more difficult matter in front of her. But that wasn't how it could be, as things were, across a three-thousand-kilometre gulf. Between her and Braun there was just too much of both sorts of distance.

Nothing for it. 'Prabha. Good to touch base. It's Hunten pol now, yes?'
'Yes.'

'Excellent. I won't keep you, this isn't a social call. I have a case with a connection to your neck of the woods.' Guerline paused, wet her lips. 'There's a body.'

FOUR

Petrakis had dressed for the meeting, more so than Othman or Bayley at any rate: the grandmother's pastel blouse and dark trousers looked freshly ironed, earrings and necklace evidently selected with care. From her jacket to her dress moccasins, Liv Petrakis presented very much as the elder professional, the slightest yet somehow most substantive of the three assembled family members. In contrast, Petrakis's daughter Paschel Othman had opted for loose-fitting grey comfortware; Tesar Bayley, Fil's grandfather, a broad-shouldered dark-skinned man with a thinning fuzz of short-cropped white hair, seemingly hadn't bothered to change out of his perspiration-shaded exercise gear. It was Scarfe's first meeting with Bayley; his demeanour, she decided, was that of someone who hoped this wouldn't take too long. Well, that made two of them.

There was something up between Paschel Othman and her parents, that much was clear from their awkwardness, their body language, their sly moodiness towards one another; but if they didn't wish to divulge what was presumably a private family matter, Guerline saw no need to push them on it. In all likelihood, it was associated with the unexpected recent return to the family nest of a grown daughter and granddaughter and the consequent upheaval of routines between the older family members. Or maybe this was just how they were at any time, standoffish and sharp. Families were odd, each one had its own atypicalities, its own behavioural blindnesses, its own red lines. Guerline knew that all too well.

She let them take their seats at the long table, smiled inwardly as they opted for a generational separation, before she sat down herself, opposite the family's tautened centre of mass. 'I'm not sure how much Filomene—Fil—has told you about her sessions with me, but they have shed light on the traumatic incident she experienced. I can answer some of your questions on that; Fil has clarified the scope of the information which she's comfortable with me passing on to you, if required. In other respects, my recommendation as always in such cases is that you otherwise wait until Fil herself wishes to discuss the matter with you, which might happen within the next few days, or alternatively might well take years. It's clear she places trust in each of you, she sees her family home as a place of safety, but that sense of safety may not extend immediately to sharing with you her concerns—her fears—about the event. I'm sure you will each have your own way of providing support to her in that. Is there anything you would like to ask, about my understanding of what it is she's been through?'

'There's a pol investigation, isn't there?' asked Othman. 'Hunten, for whatever reason it might fall to them.' Hers was a lecturer's voice, tuned for reach, well audible throughout the meeting room and perhaps somewhat beyond it.

'There is an investigation, yes,' replied Guerline. 'But my impression is that Fil won't be required for contact for that. Hunten pol have the information they need from her; the investigation will take its course from there.'

'She found some remains, out near Owen? While she was skidbiking? With a friend?' asked Tesar Bayley: more soft-spoken, reedy where his daughter's voice was brassy. Guerline hadn't checked on what the grandfather's vocation had been, and now she was curious. Less highly educated than the women, or perhaps just less accustomed to stating his opinion. Or perhaps he'd simply fallen into a default intonation which made each statement a question. 'This happened about a month ago?'

'Almost four weeks ago, yes, and a few hundred kilometres east of Owen. But the remains clearly date from some time earlier, perhaps years earlier. The pol investigation will seek to establish their origin.'

There were few further questions from Othman or Bayley, and none from the frowning and pale-faced Petrakis, so Scarfe soon moved on to the meeting's other purpose. 'This is also an opportunity to consult with you on how best the department, and Trafton, can support Fil in her recovery from trauma; not so much in regard to material assistance, but in the matter of support services, counselling, further consultation by careworkers or mental-wellness retrainers with Fil or with any of you as required. We can set up a program to support her return to work, or to track towards a different occupation if that would be preferred; she may alternatively wish to manage her reintegration into wider society entirely under your steam. It's important that you have some familiarity with the options available, as well as Fil herself of course; she may well seek your advice on this. In this regard, I can give you details of the services routinely available, but families can also have insight into gaps or omissions in coverage provided by those services, and this meeting is an opportunity for you to share such insight with me. I'll pass along any recommendations you might make, noting that decisions on those recommendations will be made by those with seniority to myself.'

There weren't any recommendations, though Paschel Othman stated that she hoped there wouldn't be undue media attention on the Hunten pol investigation. 'That's the last thing Fil needs, she really wants to put this behind her,' said Othman, turning towards her parents as though in challenge. 'I'm sure we all do.'

Guerline agreed, and the meeting concluded shortly after. As the family members filed out of the meeting room—Paschel Othman with some sense of urgency, Fil's maternal grandparents more sedately—Scarfe found herself wondering why the grandmother had taken such care with her appearance, such an effort to exert physical presence.

A matter of dignity, perhaps. But throughout the meeting, Liv Petrakis had not said one word.

*

21

Two days elapsed. Scarfe closed an unrelated case, prepared for a new one: the family of an early-onset dementia sufferer, whose condition had uncharacteristically failed to respond to the implants. Such cases were often confronting: there was a tendency for families in such circumstances to look to assign blame, when often such treatment failures were genuinely matters of ill-chance. Thorough preparation would be needed to ensure she could best address the family members' needs. She figured the Fil Bayley matter was as good as closed, now that she had effectively handed it on to Hunten pol. There'd be an exit interview with Fil, perhaps a referral to a therapy service, and she could finish the writeup.

It didn't happen that way. Prabha Braun called. An extensive search, by an uncrewed aerial vehicle, of the area in which Fil's testimony had placed the 'damaged human remains' had failed to locate the body, or even the immobilised skidbike. Was Guerline able to vouch for the reliability of the witness?

Guerline was. She was in no doubt that Fil's account of the incident was substantively correct, though it was possible that the recollection of some aspects might be inaccurate. There was no mistaking the sincerity and substantial distress with which Fil Bayley had described the sequence of events. The skidbike had hit an object protruding slightly through a level patch of ice; the impact, at speed, had damaged the bike's front skid and had sent bike and rider flying for a short distance. Bayley's companion had ridden off; Fil had walked back to the impact point to see what she'd hit. There'd been a body, a human body, a not fully complete human body embedded, frozen solid and lying more or less sideways, within the ice; the protrusion constituted a shoulder and most of an arm. The skid had caught at the elbow, had snapped the wrist; the hand stayed stuck within the ice. There'd been a head to the body, too, presumably, once, but if any of that remained, it was only in the form of a smeared stain along the ice, a marker of the passage of some previous and much heavier vehicle, though the trackway appeared to be very sparsely used, and lacked signage. The collision was real, Bayley's terror at inspecting the incident's site was genuine: therefore there was a body; but Hunten pol had not found it.

Was Prabha Braun able to confirm they'd been looking in the correct area?

This, said Braun, frowning, was why they needed to talk with Fil Bayley.

Guerline rearranged the open documents on her display, deactivated a couple of 'pending' flags. Sighed. 'Could you not get the location from the metadata in her T-suit?'

'We don't have the T-suit,' said Braun. 'We'd seek a warrant for it, but from our information it travelled back to Trafton with Bayley. It's not clear why, she wouldn't have needed it on either end of the railpod routes, neither Hunten to Woltjer nor Woltjer to Trafton.' Braun's voice made it sound like an accusation.

'She'd made a horrific discovery,' Scarfe answered. 'She associates that discovery with her time in Hunten, so she's retreated from that. I don't get the sense she's contemplating the resumption of her job there; she's done with Hunten, and with HRM. I think she sees this as a full break. From that angle, it makes sense that she'd bring the suit back with her.'

'But then it makes sense that she'd bring the bike back too, one way or another,' Prabha protested. 'Whereas she abandoned the bike. I could understand that if it was a thirty-year-old model, a Volker Trailfinder or some such, but this was a Xu Powerglide, barely two years old. That's not something most people would walk away from, regardless of the damage it had sustained. It's certainly not something I'd walk away from.'

'She was in crisis when the accident happened. She could leave the bike, so she did. She couldn't leave the suit, so she didn't. They're not the same decision, and they weren't made at the same time. These things don't always look rational from the outside, but I think her reactions are consistent overall. And probably she was fearful that she would see the bike as a continual reminder of an incident which, I can assure you as her caseworker, she found highly traumatic and is well keen to put behind her.'

'Of course. But you can appreciate this leaves us with a problem. We could find this site with her help, or with the suit, or with the bike. But we don't have any of those.'

'There's the other party,' said Scarfe. 'Aldous Fischetti, the friend, the companion. The one who took off and abandoned her. Can't he confirm—'

'That's just it, he can't.'

'How so?'

'This is in confidence. He claims no memory of the incident. And before you ask the obvious question, we've checked his suit, his bike, his slate: all of them have been stripped of recent location data. We have our suspicions as to why he might have chosen to do that, which I'm not at liberty to disclose. But you can see why we need to raise this with Bayley. Otherwise, we've no proof that any of this occurred.'

'I'm personally convinced it did. I'm used to people lying to me; I haven't read any of that in the consultations I've had with Fil. She's been reluctant to discuss some aspects, certainly, but...'

'Has she described the location to you?'

'She's described the situation. That's what's been relevant from my perspective. The scene, the reactions. The consequences for her wellbeing. There's considerable detail in what she's disclosed, her speed at the time of the accident, her concern that Fischetti's bike, trailing hers, was also going to hit the obstacle. But no, I don't have a location on this,' said Scarfe, closing a document which could wait until tomorrow. 'I can ask if she'd be available for a remote interview. She might or might not require that I'm present for it. Would that pose any problems?'

'Don't see why. She's not suspected of anything—I mean in a purely legal sense the incident probably qualifies as interfering with human remains, but it's fairly clear there was no intent in that direction, just ill chance. If she needs you to sit in, I can't see any objection. But don't seek to speak on her behalf, obviously.'

'Of course. Alright, I'll see when will suit her, and... wait, surely there's another way you can find this site. She mentioned an abandoned dwelling a few kilometres away. That should narrow it down, there can't be that many abandoned structures in that part of western Xanadu.'

'There aren't any,' said Braun. 'Not that are marked on the maps, at any rate. And nothing that showed up on the UAV's radar run. We might have better luck with a visual survey, but daylight is still three days away.'

FIVE

Say what one might against Hunten pol's ability to find human remains and a damaged skidbike somewhere along the tholin-dusted ice separating the settlement from that of Owen, but there was no faulting the pol's remote comms services. It was exactly as though Officer Braun and Agent Mashaka O'Meeghan were seated across the conference table from Scarfe and Bayley, and not so far afield that the dawn now spreading across the dunes and icefields surrounding Trafton was still two daycycles in Hunten's future.

Fil was uneasy, which was fully understandable. Braun and her associate—a birdlike, rheum-eyed man of middle years, somehow Prabha's junior, with thinning grey hair and a thick farside accent—also seemed uneasy, and Scarfe couldn't fathom that.

'Nobody is accusing you of insincerity,' said Braun, mere seconds after O'Meeghan had as good as done just that. 'But you have described features which are simply not visible.'

'It's a well-travelled route,' persisted O'Meeghan. 'Is it perhaps possible that—'

'But it's *not* a well-travelled route,' said Fil Bayley.

'We're quibbling over traffic densities now,' said O'Meeghan.

'I'm not convinced that we are,' said Guerline, turning to Bayley. 'Fil, if these officers are able to show you on a map the region searched—'

'It would be inappropriate to share evidentiary material relevant to the investigation,' said O'Meeghan.

'If you haven't found the body, let alone the bike,' said Guerline, 'I'd hesitate to describe this as an investigation. Prabha…' She paused, momentarily at a loss for how to say *please rein in your officious junior colleague* without inflaming matters further.

'I think we can agree to show them the map,' said Braun. 'Mashaka, please share the map with the UAV's radar-track overlay.'

O'Meeghan grumbled, but made some adjustments on his own device before porting an image to the tabletop's shared section. 'View only,' he said, his tone suggesting he found even this minimal level of access to be an affront to his professionalism.

Fil leaned forward, took—Scarfe presumed—several seconds to orient herself. Then she sat up; sat back. 'You're looking on the wrong iceway.'

'That's not possible,' said O'Meeghan. 'You say this happened on the track between Owen and Hunten. There's only one iceway.'

'No,' said Fil. 'There's not.'

There was no word from Braun for the next week, so Scarfe inferred that the Hunten pol now had the information they'd needed from Fil Bayley. It gave her time to concentrate on managing the competing needs of the early-onset dementia sufferer's family, who couldn't agree on the depth or the nature of medical/social support to seek. There were new cases too, as many as Scarfe felt able to take on (which was never as many as she felt she should be taking on, but then she was by no means the only caseworker in the department; and if the need were truly pressing, surely the department could look to recruitment): a young family impacted by phloo addiction, an elderly man for whom a decades-old cryowound had propagated recent and debilitating neural and muscle damage, a chronically ill mother… Guerline had the feeling she was helping these people, somewhat; she was intruding on their lives, somewhat; she was missing some point with each of them; she was gaining something through her involvement with each of these clusters of impacted or troubled people, but did that mean they were thereby losing something through the transaction? This was the cost of the work, sometimes it felt useful, sometimes it was principally a drain on her energy, and always there were other issues too: Nikita staring his approaching adolescence in the face and wondering what to make of it; the still-strained interaction with Sunder, more negotiation than dialogue; occasional social evenings with Kim and Shariq, or with the parents of some of Nik's classmates. Dates, rarely, never leading anywhere; she wasn't truly interested, it was just an action taken to dissuade her mother, and Neve, from being too persistent. It went on, all of it, the work done and the work not yet done and the socialising and the parenting, and the periodic blissful episodes of solitude. It was enough and sometimes it was slightly too much, but overall it wasn't a bad situation to be in, and Guerline was on the whole glad that Kalinda had reeled her back into the workforce those two years ago.

It was Kite Day in the largest of Trafton's weather rooms, down in the settlement's sub-basement entertainment centre: a purposefully irregular breeze had been established, cartoonish white clouds scudded across the dazzlingly blue ceiling, the facility's responsive floor had been programmed 'for the texture of a grassy meadow', and a trio of mounds—carefully spaced, Guerline was sure, to minimise the probability of kite entanglement between participants—had been raised near the chamber's windward wall. The airflow was unsettling: a life indoors had imbued in Guerline a largely subconscious sensitivity to air movement. Too little meant a failure of circulation, too much meant a leak, either meant danger. She attempted to shrug off her unease; it didn't seem as if anyone else around her was similarly fazed.

She and Nik sat, for the moment, with other parents and children at one of the two craft tables just inside the entrance, constructing their kites from the provided materials—polymer sheeting, foam-cored C-fibre dowel, soft-touch nylon cord and adhesive—while awaiting their respective turns on the mounds. It didn't escape Guerline's attention that most of the other children were younger than Nik, sometimes by several years; while his enjoyment of the freestyle craft activity appeared genuine, she suspected it wouldn't be long before such pastimes were deemed juvenile and were accordingly discarded as, perhaps, he would seek also to discard his parents, or at least the perception of their social hold over him while he touted for fickle peer approval.

Sunder had approached her recently to discuss a lock licence for Nik. It was agreed that they would share the costs for any such process; it wasn't agreed by Guerline that the boy was yet ready for this. Authority to operate an airlock, independent of parental oversight, was an important milestone on the journey towards full adulthood; but honestly, Nik didn't seem troubled. It wasn't their child who was pushing this, the drive appeared to have come from Sunder, or perhaps from Pirra. Not that Guerline was going to venture into an argument with them on the subject, but there was the not inconsiderable cost of the training program, as well as the consideration that Nik was almost certainly owed another growth spurt, which would mean the acquisition of a new T-suit, ideally one with the flexibility to last him into full adulthood… she was irritated that Sunder had raised this, and was uncertain how best to respond.

Then it was their turn on the mounds. Nik seemed suddenly self-conscious, perhaps unconvinced his kite would remain intact while aloft. Guerline suspected her own grounds for uncertainty on that front were stronger: she'd been sparing with the adhesive, at least by the standards of the five- or six-year-old who'd been seated on her other side at the craft table. They took their respective places, facing into the wind. Nik's construction took tentative flight. Guerline readied herself.

Her slate thrummed. She'd set it for 'emergencies only'. Sunder, most likely. She reached into her pocket.

It wasn't Sunder. It was Fil. She looked upset.

The craft table was no place to take a private call.

SIX

'We need archaeologists,' said Braun. O'Meeghan laughed at that, his exhalation steaming the briefing room's still-cold air. 'I'm not even joking,' Braun added.

'Where are we going to find an archaeologist in Hunten?' asked O'Meeghan. 'For that matter, where on Titan?'

'I've no idea. But those are the skills we need here, and someone will have them. If not within Hunten—or Owen would be just as good, given where we are—then not too much further afield.'

'How are you suggesting we find these people? Assuming they exist?'

'I would start with the universities and advanced vocational colleges. They'll know if any professional organisations exist for the field, locally or across the broader region. Look, it wouldn't even need to be archaeologists, there are other domains that might be useful. Conservators, restoration experts, sculptors even. Anyone with steady hands, excellent fine motor skills, good judgment and an abundance of patience. But my gut tells me archaeologists would be best, someone who can do the work in a suit. That's what the task most closely aligns itself with.'

'Your gut tells you this?'

'My instinct, then. My professional experience, if you insist.'

'I'll make enquiries,' said O'Meeghan, in a tone of voice which as good as stated he'd do so without hope of success. 'Anything else?'

'Happy to entertain your suggestions on alternative approaches.'

O'Meeghan shrugged, rose from the collapsible chair in the hab's cramped briefing room.

They'd arrived onsite one standard day ago, shipped out from Hunten, in the first few hours of the week-long Titanian day, in a pol cargo copter: not the smoothest method of transport, but it had got them here much faster than would've been possible overland. The support crew had stayed long enough to ensure that the field hab was inflated, airtight, and securely attached to the insulated waffle-frame base; that the heating and life-support systems were functional; that the prefab transmission tower was securely anchored and active; and that Adewale's precious instrumentation was as intact as a cursory check could verify. Then the copter had returned home, and it was just the three of them out here, among the frozen dead and the rotten burnt-metal stink of warmed Titan which inevitably, with repeated use, got past the airlocks into the living and working compartments. They had provisions for a week. That had seemed unnecessarily generous at the outset; with what they'd learnt in the hours since, it now looked as manifestly insufficient as the living-space within what the field hab's designers had optimistically described as a three-person environment.

In the quarters she shared with Adewale, Braun kept the heating down, the air circulation ramped up. She'd learnt from experience that this was the fastest way to dissipate the Titan tholin taint from the air. She'd also learnt from experience that the no-frills circulation system on a hab like this would ensure the odour was shunted from room to room to room a good few times before being properly purged, by which time anyone's use of the airlock would bring in olfactory reinforcements.

Hardcopies of the latest ice-penetrating radar drone runs over the site lay on the desk before her: confusing smears of heightened colour overlaid with a grid and with sporadic numbers which presumably meant something to those who knew how to read such maps. The hardcopies weren't Prabha Braun's preference—she would rather take the old-school approach, slate displays and, when needed, holoprojections—but O'Meeghan's justification was that the physical objects better crystallised his ability to analyse. *Well then*, thought Prabha, *crystallise away*. But Mashaka O'Meeghan was stuck, it seemed, in the problem's enormity; as was Braun herself. It was just too large a quantity of ice to contend with; and a quantity, too, of uncertain structural integrity.

The problem wasn't the first body, the child's, which had been partially protruding from the ice surface and which Fil Bayley had so traumatically discovered in the skidbike incident. They'd removed that, as intact as possible, through standard crime-scene excavation techniques, and Adewale was currently doing whatever she customarily did with such remains, gathering whatever evidence she could on the boy's demise and botched interment. The conundrum they now faced, Braun and O'Meeghan onsite, and the other pol officers assigned to the case back in Hunten, was the array of other bodies buried deeper within the ice. The IPR sweeps suggested there were seven, but O'Meeghan had hinted it might conceivably be more; the signal was grainy, the ice itself was opaque, and it was near-impossible to determine, by scanning, whether there were more bodies further beneath those the radar had revealed.

The means of burial had been simplicity itself, if somewhat resource-wasteful; but then the graves' engineers likely hadn't used ultrapurified water as the flooding agent. It was a method not these days regarded as best practice; in some jurisdictions, it was now banned outright. Still, the approach had been used fairly widely on Titan, in years past, for those families who chose against, or the settlements which forbade, chemical rendering or cremation: dig a hole of sufficient depth in the ice using standard excavation methods, or even—if there weren't, say, other remains buried in marked graves in the vicinity—create one using explosives; then place the body, in a weighted and sealed coffin, within the hole; then flood it with water and wait the few hours necessary for the burial pool to freeze solid. Here they hadn't even bothered with the prior excavation, nor the coffins: it appeared they had simply placed the bodies, weighted in some manner, and (as suggested by the child's example) clothed but otherwise unprotected from the elements, at a deep enough spot in a dry streambed. Perhaps they'd needed to dam up one or both ends of the section chosen, before inundating the hollow with several tonnes of water, enough to cover all the bodies to a depth of a metre or more, enough water that it would've taken several hours to completely freeze through. No care had been taken, it seemed, to place the bodies separately from each other: they'd overlapped, arms sprawled across a neighbour's chest or legs. Or so O'Meeghan had inferred from the drone's still-ongoing scans of the site.

All up, it was a mess; all up, it bore the characteristics of a mass grave. More a dumping than a burial.

Sometime in those first few still-liquid hours, the child's body had come free of its weights, had risen to the surface, had pierced whatever ice had formed atop the pool; and this had been the tableau which had frozen. Prabha wondered at that: that this disruption must have happened very soon after the site's flooding, and yet had not been noticed, or at least had not been addressed, by any of those who'd been responsible for the interment. It spoke of a scene very swiftly departed. It spoke of haste, of negligence, of disrespect.

It spoke of a crime.

Seven bodies, eight bodies, nine bodies; perhaps yet more. Unrecorded, unregarded. How had they died? They'd been interred together: had they died together? And how long had they lain there?

Someone had known what they were doing, with this callous disposal. Someone might still know. Prabha was determined to track down that person, those persons, if they still drew breath.

She'd sat long enough; she needed to stretch her legs. Time to suit up.

They'd fenced the gravesite, more to mark it than to secure it. The makeshift perimeter served to define the problem they faced. It wasn't a large expanse of ice: only about five metres by two, including the metre-wide pit from which they had already excavated the ice encasing the child's body. It took Braun less than half a minute to circumnavigate at a slow, respectful, introspective pace.

It wasn't immediately obvious, without the perimenter markings, where the newer ice segued into the pre-existing terrain: rust-dark windblown dust, small grains of the sootlike tholins that sooner or later covered everything on Titan, had stained the surface; and the new and the older ice alike had been sparsely scored by the trackmarks and runnels which resulted from infrequent vehicular traffic. Who had known to use this route, that was not mapped, and why had they done so? It was one of many as yet unanswered questions.

Consider the way the mass grave's unidentified creators had inundated this short stretch of the streambed: it seemed they must have just dumped the water over the bodies, through a wide-bore pipe or some such contrivance, in a matter of minutes; likely the pipe would have been heated itself, to prevent getting ice-clogged. A smaller pipe, a slower rate of flow, would have caused the added water to freeze more quickly over and around the dumped bodies, something which the child's tragic buoyancy argued against. (Prabha had wondered at that buoyancy: absent the waste gases resulting from decomposition, a consideration which very likely didn't apply here, why had the boy's body risen to the surface at all? Kordell's hypothesis was that, with the water freezing from the ground up, a sufficiently large floe of submerged ice could have carried the body, presumably the smallest of those present, with it to the surface when it broke free.) Aside from the buoyancy issue, the engineering aspect of the flooding process wasn't a difficult aspect, and perhaps not in itself an important one, for the investigation: there were no material traces of the equipment used, but it might not have assisted Braun and the others greatly had there been. The speed, again, spoke to a hasty disposal process.

Perhaps they'd been a family group, off-gridding it out here, the ones now buried within an ultra-cold matrix of ice: slain as part of a decades-old, even centuries-old vendetta; it had happened elsewhere. Or perhaps they'd held, or had been imagined to have held, a key of some sort to mineral wealth, and had been killed in a brutal greed-fuelled assault. There were precedents for both scenarios, and likely a good many more as well. They were still missing too much of the necessary information.

There was a more subtle aspect. Were the investigators to attempt to excavate the encasing ice in one piece, it would likely mean needing to hew out a fifty-tonne chunk. This might ultimately be doable—her engineering friend, Talvi who worked in construction, would have a good idea of the task's feasibility—but it would be a slow and difficult process, which was what had led Prabha to contemplate the opposing method of painstakingly digging down to each body in sequence, following the expert guidance of those practised in such an approach (or at least its analogues). Fifty tonnes of field-contaminated water ice was a lot, but probably a majority of this would be from the banks of the streambed, the pre-existing substrate which had acted as the mould for the ice-tomb. Plausibly the amount of liquid water that had been dumped in was a much smaller quantity: twelve, fifteen, twenty tonnes. They'd know the exact amount sooner or later. But even twelve tonnes of liquid water, regardless of its purity, was a not-inexpensive commodity: it carried considerable cost nowadays, and it would definitely have been costly whenever this burial had occurred. A typical household budget, in a medium-sized settlement or arcology, ran to between three and five tonnes of accessible water at any one time, with a fraction of that meeting food-safety standards and the rest in various stages of the repurification cycle. Twelve tonnes was a lot; it seemed unlikely any off-grid household would have access to that much. The dumping might even have involved twice that quantity; O'Meeghan didn't yet have a good indication on the streambed's depth at that point.

So: flood the site, quickly and without apparent regard for material expense, then flee the scene within hours, probably within minutes, before the dead boy's final short journey to the pool's freezing surface. With all of this happening in a wilderness location, not on any marked route and in proximity only to an abandoned and seemingly gutted structure which didn't appear on any records.

Clearly that abandoned structure was overdue a visit. She'd get O'Meeghan to suit up, once she'd checked in with Adewale. Some time properly in the field would do the agent good.

*

Crime's nature in the larger settlements was different to that pertaining within the smaller arcologies and habitats: Hunten crime was urbanised, resulting from the frictions and grievances and opportunities which heaped up when substantial numbers of people were grouped together within a comparatively confined environment. Several of the other officers within Hunten pol held seniority over Braun, in a technical sense, but that seniority was largely derived from experience in combatting crime within the settlement's living spaces: commercial fraud, corruption, domestic tragedies, urbanised outbursts of intoxicant-fuelled violence and the like. In this sense, Braun's experience in field investigation was a rarity, and it was for this reason (she thought) that she'd been placed in nominal charge of securing whatever evidence the site might hold, aided by O'Meeghan's instrumental expertise and by Kordell Adewale, the forensic pathologist who had been her colleague at Turtle pol, and who had applied in parallel with Braun to join Hunten pol when, in an administrative streamlining, the small pol force at Turtle was retrenched and partially subsumed by that at neighbouring Hepburn. Braun had parents, mother and stepfather, in Hunten, which simplified the need for childminding when work made unavoidable demands on her time, as it did now. Later she learned also that Lassa's other grandmother, Laszlo's mother, now lived there too, which overall was a good thing also. She wasn't sure what had guided Adewale's choice in applying for one of the vacant positions here.

The site investigation was only one thread in a braided process. Ngata and Whiteneck were compiling a list of unresolved missing-person cases from Hunten and environs, dating back to the settlement's establishment almost a century ago; Quinn Saitō was painstakingly working through the historical records of the Hunten Regional Development Office to establish details of the abandoned site's operations and active period, thus far without any apparent success; others were involved in related tasks of which Braun wasn't directly aware.

She padded along the corridor to the pathology lab, bracing herself for the chamber's expected chill. In fact the door opened onto a temperate environment; and Adewale was leaning over a stereoscopic microscope, not elbows-deep into the heavily insulated glovebox in which the inquisition of the boy's remains had been occurring this past day. Indeed, the glovebox's cryo compartment was now empty; but surely Kordell hadn't finished with the body already?

'Come in,' said Kordell on perceiving Braun's approach.

'What have you done with our headless friend?' asked Prabha.

'Kuiper. I've taken all the necropsies that are justified for the moment, but we still don't know whether the boy died from injury, whether accidental or intentional, or from some medical condition. I'm hoping to get some of that from the bloodwork and tissue assays, but we need a detailed internal scan, full body—don't say it—to get a more complete picture. So he's been shipped off to Kuiper for magnetic resonance imaging.'

'Surely we can access that back in Hunten?'

'Not with deep cryo during the scan. I want to preserve the cold chain on this to the full extent possible, to ensure we don't lose any clues among the volatiles. And Kuiper and Sagan are the two places on-world which do deep cryo MRI.'

'Wouldn't Sagan be closer?'

'There's precious little in it. Really, it comes down to backlog and paperwork, and Kuiper wins out on both. But come and look at this.' Adewale gestured an image onto the wallscreen beside the microscope stand. A grid of some sort, imperfectly regular; bulky loops of a reddish brown. Fabric, Prabha realised. She was looking at a highly magnified view of a scrap of thick fabric. Coarse and messy.

'Is this a sample from what the child was wearing?'

Kordell nodded. 'It's not machine made.'

'I can tell that. But what's the significance?'

'Someone loved this lad enough to knit him a sweater.'

'Does this help us?'

'Perhaps. It's not real wool, of course; it's a synthetic. In all likelihood, it was dyed during the manufacturing process; and from what I understand, that's generally a small-batch operation. There will be slight differences in dye tone and composition from batch to batch. It's likely I can date the batch: someone, somewhere, will have records of the relevant details, because there's always someone who obsesses about a field like this. Which gives us a proxy, an unreliable one admittedly, for this poor kid's year of death.'

'It could be a hand-me-down,' said Prabha.

'Yes, that's true. But it would be a place to start looking. The year of death can't be further back than the year of the batch's manufacture.'

'And that year is?'

'If I knew that, Prabha, I'd have told you already. I'm not a yarn-analysis expert, I'm feeling my way through this. It'll most likely be another day or so before I can get that nailed down. And when I do, you'll be the second to know.'

'No ballpark in the interim?'

'Nothing useful. Cryo is as close to stasis as we can get, so there's sod-all evidence of change to look for, and there are too many untidy variables for a rate-of-surface-deposition analysis to tell us anything more than that this dates back within the last century or two, which we obviously knew from the outset. But my gut tells me this is old. Decades.'

'Mine too,' said Braun. 'Listen, I'm going to take O'Meeghan along to check out the local ruins. Want to tag?'

'I'll pass. But let me know if you find anything needs checking out.'

From the outside, the building was bland and uninviting: tholin-streaked on a side facing the prevailing winds, mid-grey on the other side visible as Prabha approached the obvious entry-point. If the surrounding ice had once been groomed for vehicular access, this had been undone by subsequent human activity, possibly by the hubbub of the site's abandonment. She ventured in, leaving O'Meeghan to learn what he could from the terrain.

From the inside, the structure appeared devoid of any indication of its former purpose. Whatever it had been, it wasn't anymore. Triple-thickness exterior walls of construction polymer, bare, essentially intact except where cables and panels had evidently been stripped out; flooring marked by the former presence of unidentifiable furniture, and scraped in places by the relocation of now-absent heavy items; the severed ends of pipes or ducts, protruding from the inner walls in a few places, marking where there had once been plumbing or heating or air purification equipment: Prabha wasn't build-familiar enough to be able to ascertain which. Doorways had been left fully open; there were no windows, which in older structures wasn't that unusual—a window was a point of vulnerability against the unforgiving environment—but it felt wrong regardless. No lighting; no remaining traces of anything electrical, anything data-driven. If there was wiring left underfloor or within the walls, it didn't emerge anywhere that she could see. In two smaller rooms, toilet bowls had been adjudged insufficiently worth the time, or the effort, to detach from the floor, though seats and lids had been removed; in one larger room, bolts protruded from the thick insulated-polymer floor, anchoring nothing. *They've stripped it clear of anything which could carry information*, she thought to herself, as her headlamps illuminated empty room after empty room. It took her perhaps five minutes to make a first cursory sweep; then she began a more methodical inspection, capturing images of whatever seemed relevant—which wasn't much.

And yet there was still information to be gleaned, if the searcher applied herself to the task. The structure was sufficiently large—a floor surface, in total, of perhaps twenty by twenty-five metres—and sufficiently distant from other settlements to imply an activity of some significance, requiring isolation or secrecy or both. The toilets and those bolts in the floor—a feature strongly suggestive of interior machinery— implied habitation, or at least storage for some commodity perishable enough to require a human-tolerable temperature regime, and a human-breathable atmosphere: this was no mere equipment shed or vehicle depot. People had lived here, people had worked here, probably several people among these almost two dozen empty rooms; this had been both home and workplace for a group of people. Bedrooms; food preparation areas; common-access areas; washrooms; workspaces: they must all have been here, but save for the two small toilet cubicles, it was no longer possible to designate the purpose of any one room. And single-storey: why? Structures on Titan were seldom built on just one level: it maximised the thermal cost to have such a large floor surface in close contact with the ultracold ice of Titan's crust. If the interior had been one large space, an expansive floorplan might have been necessitated, for whatever reason might apply to that circumstance, but this place could easily have been configured as a three- or four-storey structure, or perhaps built on stilts; it would surely have been cheaper and safer to run.

And what had befallen the building's occupants? Were all the members of that group those who were now buried in the ice-filled gully a kilometre or so westward?

Surely not all of them; for who would have done the entombing, the dismantling?

Whoever had been here, whoever had abandoned this, had gone against one key part of Titan's social compact: when you departed a structure, left it empty, you left it essentially intact, whether all of those systems essential for survival were properly functional; you left the requirements for life-support in place, so the non-functioning components could be repaired or replaced if need be, if it became the case that the structure or dwelling was sought as a haven by those requiring it, perhaps having become lost or stranded or otherwise in need in Titan's hinterlands. Of course there were those who flouted this aspect of the social compact, who when they found a structure waiting empty would pillage or trash it, to a greater degree or smaller; that was unavoidable, that was human nature, it couldn't be guarded against. But that wasn't what had happened here, that was apparent from the too-tidy emptiness of this abandoned building: it had been gutted in an impressively systematic fashion. Even the airlocks had been removed, leaving breaches in the exterior walls on opposite side of the building, and what reason would anyone have to do that?

If the structure itself knew, it wasn't letting on.

She returned to the entrance, her head brimming with questions.

O'Meeghan called from outside, loud, as much suit-muffled audio as radio: he'd found something. A skidbike with a broken front sled.

So Fil Bayley has been here, Prabha noted.

The skidbike was lying on the tholin-smudged ice at an inward-facing corner of the building's outer wall; but it was the corner, not the bike, which drew Prabha's interest. She briefly explored the adjacent wall sections and returned to the corner where the bike lay. 'That's different,' she said.

'What do you mean?' asked O'Meeghan.

'This.' She pointed into the corner. 'Inside, the building is just a rectangle overall, there's a corridor around the outside, with rooms inward, some interconnecting, some not, but the corridor just runs straight along each outer wall, and there are no rooms off to the outside. Here, there's an add-on, an extra room.'

'You must've missed the doorway.'

'I doubt it. I went through twice. The doors have all been left fully open, or in some cases removed entirely. Like the airlocks.'

'Let's check,' said O'Meeghan. 'But give me a leg up first. I want to check the roof. I tried to get a vantage from that ridge to the south, but it's not high enough. I can see that there are a few features on the roof, but I couldn't make them out properly.'

'Should've brought the drone,' Prabha commented. O'Meeghan agreed that he should have, then nodded theatrically toward the roof. She laced her glove fingers together, cradle-fashion, crouched, then straightened up once he had shifted his weight to his raised foot. The servoes did most of the lifting for her, but she was nonetheless surprised how limber he still was, how sure of his ability to haul himself atop the building's flat roof, fully three and a half metres above ground level.

She shook her fingers, to the extent possible: the servoes hadn't done all of the lifting for her.

'D'you want video?' he asked in her earbud.

'No, please, that always gives me motion sickness. Just static images. And map anything of interest.'

'That won't take long. There are just a couple of vents: could be thermal, could be waste gases. Kordell might have a better idea.'

'She can maybe interpret the images,' Prabha suggested. 'You okay to jump down when you're done, or do I have to play at the human ladder once more?'

'No, should be right.'

O'Meeghan was right, re the doorway to the extra room; she had missed it on her earlier inspection. Two floor-to-ceiling panels, each a metre wide, nearly but not quite flush with, and nearly but not quite a colour match with, the rest of the corridor's outer wall. The panels gave a hollow echo when rapped with the knuckles of her glove, or at least spoke of a level of solidity different to that of the rest of the corridor wall.

A standard pressure-seal sliding door, by all appearances. But it was sealed tight, and if there had been a control panel to either side of the double doors, or on the facing wall, it had been removed along with everything else. When pushed against, there was give in the door, but only towards the top; the bottom was jammed fast, or braced, or something. Even with both of them trying at once, their gloves' servoes straining with the effort, they couldn't push either door far enough in to engage the slide mechanism. It might have been broken; might have been sabotaged.

If they applied a different order of brute force, it would probably be possible to break through, but that didn't feel right. It could hardly be said that there was urgency, investigating an abandoned site like this, a kilometre from a historical burial; and there would probably be as much chance of destroying evidence as of finding it.

'Can you hotwire it?' she asked him.

'If there's an identifiable control point in the wall anywhere, yes. But I didn't bring the tools I'd need with me. And I don't think there's enough left to attach an override to—they've been very thorough in stripping the site.'

'There has to be a way through.'

'There will be, but it'll require effort and time. Are we even sure this place is connected with the remains?'

'My instinct—sorry, my professional experience—tells me it must be. I would've thought yours did too.'

'Probably it does,' he said, and she thought he sounded tired.

They went back outside.

'It's about three metres square,' said Prabha. 'That's a three-by-three room we can't get into.'

'Waste disposal, perhaps. Or hazardous goods storage. That's what that kind of configuration suggests.'

'Why not just storage generally?'

'Could be. Though they'd probably not be able to fit in everything out of the other rooms, so we probably shouldn't get our hopes up too much about what's inside it. If they've gone to considerable lengths to conceal the bodies, they've presumably removed or destroyed anything else that would be incriminating. Whatever it is that happened here. Has Kordell found any signs of violence on the boy's body?'

'I think that's difficult to assess, given the amount of… damage sustained post-mortem. She was hoping an MRI would help, but that'll take days from the sound. In the meantime, it'd be good to know what's behind this door.'

'We can catheter it,' he suggested. 'Where there's a join, there's a gap. We can feed a fibre-optic cable through, and scope it out that way. Failing that, I can drill an aperture for the cable.'

'Do we have that kind of equipment on hand?'

'I've got something which will do it,' said O'Meeghan. 'I'll tend to it next trip.'

They were on their way back from the abandoned structure. The earpiece in Prabha's helmet chirped. Adewale.

'You've got something?'

'Depends. How good's your poker face?'

'I've no idea what you mean.'

'I've timed the event. Fifty-eight point six standard years ago, plus or minus fifteen weeks.'

'You got this how?'

'Image search, on media images showing a boy in a handknitted sweater of that size and that precise dye mix. There were three hits, all consistent for that timing, and two of them a close match for the boy's apparent phenotype. Which means I also have a name.'

'And?'

'Poker face, please. I'm serious. The boy's name was Nils O'Meeghan.'

SEVEN

Delfranco's was sufficiently busy that it was difficult finding a table for two. Guerline seated herself and waited, scanning the customers while she ladled a heaped teaspoon of sugar into her espresso, wondering whether this was a good idea. Surrounding her, the animated hubbub of caffeine-fuelled (and caffeine-anticipating) conversation. A meeting in her office would have been more private, more discreet. More professional. A meeting at Fil's mother's dwelling, or at her grandparents', would have been less formal.

But a meeting in her office, or on home ground, wasn't what Fil Bayley had wanted.

Fil arrived: plainly anxious, troubled. Frowned as she looked around. Noticed Scarfe. The frown didn't exactly vanish.

'What would you like?' Guerline asked, once the other had taken the seat opposite her. 'My shout.'

'Tea, grey if they've got it,' said Fil, voice sufficiently small that Guerline had to reach to catch it. 'No sweetener.' Tea was ordered.

'So,' said Guerline, and waited. Strove to make herself as unthreatening as possible.

'I've— there's a problem. I need to go to Hunten to collect the skidbike.'

'And?'

'There's something I kept from the, from Braun, when we spoke. I think I forgot it at the time, but—'

'You *think* you forgot it? You're not sure whether this was accidental or deliberate? I'm not judging, I'm just trying to understand.'

'It's been difficult,' said Fil, and the frown of her mouth deepened. 'I just want advice, I think. I told Ma about it, and I think that was a mistake. I...'

Guerline took a last draught of her espresso, placed the still-warm tumbler on the tabletop in front of her. Met Fil's worried expression, waited a few seconds to see if there was more. 'In my experience,' she said slowly, 'the p— those people are generally quite understanding if you're upfront with having neglected to mention something earlier. Providing you approach them with it, rather than wait for them to raise it with you as a gap in what you've told them.'

'It's not,' Fil began; stalled. 'It's not a gap in what I told them. It's something I took.'

'From the cr—' Guerline interrupted herself, mindful of the customers at neighbouring tables. 'From the place where it happened?'

'Yes. Well, no, but close enough.'

It was Guerline's turn to frown. 'I don't follow.'

'From the derelict site.'

'You didn't tell me you'd been there. You said you walked from the site to the Huygens-Hunten trackway, a three-hour walk in near-full darkness, and you were picked up by an ore hauler two hours later.'

'That part's correct. But it was the skidbike. I could've dragged that to the main trackway, it would've taken longer but it would've been manageable, but I couldn't be sure I could get a lift which would have space to take the bike as well. I didn't want to leave it lying roadside on a busy route like that, it'd be asking for it to get smashed or stolen. And I didn't want to just leave it at the... you know. I couldn't. Not there with that. I had to move it somewhere. And it was just a kilometre or so to the derelict building; it was on the way to the main trackway, or close enough. So I left it there. There was a corner, tucked in around the back sort of. But as I was dragging the bike around toward the corner, the skid's stump dislodged something from the ice, something small and pale. I was worried, after what had happened, that it was a piece of bone. But it wasn't.'

'What was it?'

Fil pulled something from her dress pocket, tabled it. 'This.' A small plastic bag, holding a translucent cylindrical polymer object, about eight centimetres in length: a vial of some sort, labelled, tholin-stained. The object looked empty; Guerline couldn't read the label through the bag and the staining.

'If it's not from the site itself, it's probably not relevant,' said Guerline. She nudged the bag back towards Fil.

Fil reversed the motion. 'I'd rather you keep it, for the moment. The way Ma reacted when I mentioned it, I don't think she wants it in the house.'

'Did she say why?'

'No, she just froze, for like ten seconds maybe. Stared at it. It was obvious she wasn't happy.'

'Do you want me to dispose of it?'

'That'd be bad, wouldn't it? If it's something important. It just feels— can you just keep it, until we've contacted Braun about it?'

Guerline placed the bag in her handbag. 'We?' she asked, frowning. She'd been an hour from closing the case when Fil's request for a meeting had come through; now she was getting pulled back in.

'I just can't,' said Fil. 'And you'd know better how to bring something like this up with them, I think.'

'I can contact Braun on your behalf,' Guerline said, placing the words with caution. 'But the account of how this happened is going to need to come from you.'

'I know. I'll explain it; I just wouldn't know where to begin.' Fil seemed belatedly to notice her glass of tea, swallowed half of it. 'Would I— is this something I'd need a lawyer for?'

'You're not suspected of anything. You don't think this is related. I can't really advise on that question, but... *do* you think this is related?'

'I don't know. Someone did that, to the boy I mean, and that building was nearby. I shouldn't have taken it, should I?'

'Was it the only… item like that there?'

'It looked like it. Not that I lingered, the light was getting really low, but it looked like the place had been picked clean. Or cleared out. Usually there's junk, empty places get left in a mess, but this one had nothing. It was a bit sinister really.' Fil stood, distracted by something. 'I'd better go.'

'We'll sort this out,' said Guerline. 'I'll call Braun, I'll make a time for you to speak with her. I can accompany you, or not.'

'Accompany would be good. Thank you.'

She returned to the office, cued things up with Prabha Braun, omitting any mention of the vial. Then she bided her time with some non-crucial case admin—the kind of thing which Kalinda had always seemed to want prioritised, though her successor didn't much seem to mind anymore about the timescale on which such things got done—while waiting until Toan had some time free.

Her supervisor looked tired, or perhaps just old. Guerline briefed her about the early-onset dementia case, and the phloo addict, before mentioning as though in passing that she would be absent for two or three days, starting the day after next.

'Doing anything exciting?' Toan asked.

'I'm accompanying Fil Bayley to Hunten. She needs to pick up her skidbike.'

Toan raised her eyebrows. 'Surely it can just be shipped to her.'

'She also needs to talk to the pol there.'

'There's a criminal issue?'

'Possibly. Not involving Bayley, but she's a witness. They're trying to establish what originally happened at the scene.'

'And this communication with the pol—it can't be conducted remotely, from here in Trafton?'

'No. There's a sequence of people who wish to speak to her, and I gather their preference in that circumstance is for personal attendance.'

'Doesn't she have a parent or guardian who could accompany her? Her mother?'

'I don't think she has that kind of relationship with her mother.'

If Toan wondered just what kind of relationship was required for vehicle collection purposes, she didn't voice this. Instead she said, 'I can't approve this as an official undertaking.'

'I'm not asking you to. I've put in a request for unpaid leave, and I'll be paying my own way.'

'It's a bit irregular.'

'She's still struggling somewhat. Outwardly she's coping, more or less, but the trauma is still there. I'm in the process of arranging professional help for her, beyond what we ourselves can offer, but a counsellor or a therapist won't provide this kind of practical support. I'm aware it doesn't fit within my position description; but she trusts me, and I can do this for her.'

'Are you saying she doesn't trust her mother?'

'It's more complicated than that.'

Toan rubbed her brow with her fingertips. 'Very well. But to be clear, we're signing Bayley out next week, yes? That's what we agreed on Monday. Of course, there can always be an extension when genuinely warranted, but barring a true emergency I don't want to see this impinging on the other parts of your caseload.'

'It won't,' Guerline assured her.

Though she knew it would.

On an afterthought, she messaged Kalinda, though it took her longer than felt justified to lay out her reasons for doing so; it was not appropriate to brief her former supervisor on the full particulars of Fil Bayley's circumstances, but it was possible Fil might yet choose to return to Hunten to take up work once again, once the past's ghosts had died down. If she did so, it would be important to have support services available, and Kalinda could certainly orchestrate those if required.

This impending trip would be an opportunity to introduce Kalinda to Fil, so she'd know who she could seek out if the need arose.

Nik was now pushing for a lock licence, quantifying at each opportune moment (and not a few inopportune ones) the numerous reasons why parental agreement on a lock safety awareness training module for their son was, really, an investment in the future for both Guerline and Sunder. This newfound interest was, it seemed, an unexpected windfall of the Kite Day outing: among the e-leaflets which he'd harvested from the weather rooms social board, there'd been one from the Trafton battlekite guild, a team of enthusiasts who met sporadically—which is to say, on days when the atmospheric conditions suited kite-flying, which was not often given the generally lacklustre nature of Titan's equatorial breezes—for displays and contests of aerial combat. There were, on occasion, hastily convened regional meets too, when the Trafton team took on their counterparts from Woltjer and Coustenis before the winds died down again. The guild's membership fee was modest, but the preconditions for the junior membership towards which Nik aspired were the formal consent of at least one parent or guardian and tenure of a Trafton lock licence in good standing.

It would be an important step in their son's social development, it would be an opportunity for him to acquire new and widely applicable technical skills, it would further his understanding of the Titanian environment in ways that his education inexplicably could not, it would provide him with exercise, and they were always telling him—were they not?—that he should get out more, should not just spend his free time playing in his room with his T-vehicle collection…

He was water on a stone on the topic, and his insistence quite nettled the generally placid Guerline. Nor did she feel she could seek allyship in Sunder, since she knew his view on the subject of the licence to be different to hers. She needed to address her son's indefatigability head-on, and did so.

'It isn't fair,' he told her. 'You get to do whatever you want.'

'I wouldn't say that I do,' she replied. 'There are quite substantial constraints placed on my actions at work, and there are responsibilities and various steps which need to be taken. I know it might look like adults have all the control, but a lot of that control is imposed from elsewhere. That's how society operates.'

'Yes, but you have a job you enjoy—'

She allowed that this was the case.

'—and you're most probably going to get to go with Fil to Hunten when she goes to pick up her skidbike.'

'What?' Guerline's limbs grew tense. 'Why— first of all, how do you happen to know that person's name? I don't talk about the specifics of any of my cases with you. With anyone, outside work.'

'Yes, but she's a friend of Hinewai's. Well, not a friend completely, but they know each other from school, and I think Fil had heard about when you helped Hinewai…'

Guerline shook her head; not in denial, but in an effort to clear it. Trafton was a mid-sized settlement, it hadn't featured in her thinking that there might be a connection of some kind between Fil Bayley and Nik's step-sister Hinewai Driscoll. Yes, the two young women must be reasonably close in age, but that would also be true for hundreds of others. And she might also have expected that Bayley would have mentioned any interactions of this type to her; it should have come out in the consultations, one way or another. It wasn't necessarily a problem, it didn't necessarily amount to a conflict, but it had led to her now being blindsided by her son… 'I'm not going to discuss this further, and I don't want you to raise this again, with me or anyone else. Fil's— that person's situation is private, and it's always important to respect a person's privacy.'

Nik looked chastened. Wrinkled brow. 'So was it wrong for Fil— for that person to have told Hinewai?'

'No. She's allowed to talk about her life, of course she is. I'm not, because of the role I have. You can understand that, can't you? And the difficulty with you talking about such things is that people may assume you've heard them from me.'

'I haven't told anyone else.'

'I appreciate that, Nik. It was mainly that I hadn't known about the connection with Hinewai.' *And Hinewai's choice to not keep the matter to herself,* but Guerline couldn't say that, it would intrude on the dynamic in the other family grouping within which Nik operated. He was a smart kid; he'd make that connection for himself. 'Now, how about we go grab some sharkstix before I take you back to your dad's?'

'But we haven't finished with the lock licence.'

'We have for now. Nik, your father and I will discuss this, but you need to give us some space to have that discussion.'

Relief, guilt, vacancy, a sense of disorientation; the usual post-dropoff feelings. But her home's door was open.

She was sure she'd closed it.

EIGHT

She would have to tell him; but this wasn't a conversation to have helmet-to-helmet.

Nor was it a discussion fit for the hab's too-confined decontam cubicle, with both of them half-clothed and turned away from each other as they dressed, while they waited for the jets of frigid air to rinse away the stink of suit removal.

She arranged a meeting in the briefing room: herself, O'Meeghan and Adewale, each of the other two looking as troubled as she herself felt; but, while she reviewed for herself the form of words which would be most appropriate, he spoke up.

'There's another dump,' he said. 'There has to be. Whatever happened here, they dumped the bodies, because they didn't want them found. But the building has been gutted: there's nothing left of whatever furniture and equipment had been there. Whatever's in the annexe, and we should know that soon enough, there's no way it has room for all the fittings from a five-hundred square metre building, even if it was stacked floor to ceiling. You can't tell me they carted all that away with them, and just took the quickest fix possible for concealing the bodies. If this was something done in haste, and it points that way, then they dumped the gear too. In another gully, most probably, because there's no trace of it in this one. I could set the drone to overfly—'

'Mashaka,' Prabha began. 'There's been a development.'

'More remains?' he asked, perhaps trying to read the seriousness of her tone.

'No. Kordell has made an identification. A tentative identification. Of one of the bodies. The boy in the ice.' She paused, waiting until he returned eye contact. 'We think he died fifty-eight years ago, and his name was Nils O'Meeghan. He was nine years old.'

He skewed his mouth. 'Well, that's a coincidence. The name.'

'No,' said Prabha. 'It's not. Mashaka, that's your cousin Nils out there.'

'I don't have a cousin Nils.'

'How can you not—' She stopped, regrouped. Shock she'd been expecting from him, or sorrow, or anger; or any blend, really, of those. Denial she hadn't. 'I don't understand.'

'I know of three cousins, all women. Clarity, Sian, Tivona. They're my mother's brother's children, and as far as I know they are still alive, though Clarity and Tivona are in Sagan now, not Hunten, so I haven't seen them in several years. This Nils—he would presumably be my uncle's son, on my father's side. They never talked, my dad and my uncle; I don't know why that was, but it was a rule in our family, that we didn't talk to or even about Uncle Willem. I have a vague recollection that we heard about his cremation, I would've been just five or six; we didn't go. I honestly did not know if he had any children. I don't remember hearing even whether he had a partner. So this Nils, no, I haven't heard of him.'

'But assuming the fact of a familial relationship is true, however estranged, that's a conflict for the investigation.'

'I don't see why it should be.'

'You're his cousin.'

'But there was no contact. I never even met him.'

'Yes, but—That's not how Sabatier is going to see it; I'm sure you know that already. Quite aside from anything else, we don't have the h— we don't have enough for a standard identification of the body. So it will have to be done via DNA. His DNA, and yours, which, if it shows relatedness, would make you a witness. You can't be both witness and investigator, not in a situation like this.'

*

Whatever else one might say of a field investigation, it was undeniable that the seating was worse. Prabha shifted her posture yet again, trying to find some approximation of comfort upon a chair which had seemingly been designed with portability its sole guiding principle. She was alone at the briefing table, devoting to the investigation some of the hours which should more properly be designated for sleep. But the foldaway cot's designer appeared to have understood even less of human anatomy than had the collapsible chair's; if she had to start the next day ill-rested, frazzled and irascible, she could at least achieve something useful in the meantime. Perhaps.

Seeking to mentally drown out the drone of the air purifier and its faint taint of haunted solder—they would have to swap out that filter soon—Braun reviewed what was publicly known of Nils O'Meeghan and his parents. Of Nils himself there was little record; in that respect, the images of the boy in the sweater were outliers. There was scarcely more on his mother, Becki; but the father, Willem O'Meeghan, had left a plentiful trail of digital breadcrumbs across almost a hemisphere of Titan, before his death in a vehicle accident—structural failure of a two-person thopter traversing the remote Adiri highlands—ten weeks after the last record of the whereabouts of his spouse and his son.

Was there a connection between the boy's fate and his mother's disappearance? The timing was suggestive. Was, perhaps, Becki Grissom one of the other bodies in the gully's seemingly impromptu ice grave? It was a possibility, but Prabha was wary of speculating on the subject. And what of Willem's death? Was it indeed accidental, as it had been adjudged at the time? It might well not be feasible to ascertain anything useful of the thopter incident's circumstances, this long after the event; nor were the Hunten pol well placed to investigate such a matter, on a jurisdictional basis. But it could clearly not be excluded that the boy's father might have been involved in the child's death, and perhaps that of his mother.

What of the other family members? Her colleague Mashaka would clearly, at age six, have been too young for any credible involvement, but the generations above him were a different matter. The brothers had been estranged—and Prabha worked and reworked that information, seeking to see where it led—but was that true of other family members? After fifty-eight years, several of the principals were dead, but two of the three cousins—which was to say Mashaka's cousins Sian Jette and Clarity Gilje—were still alive. She could start with them: as junior members of Mashaka's mother's side of the family, their relationship with his father's brother might well have been slight, but they may have information as to the depth and the breadth of the rift between the brothers, and perhaps even its substance.

It was a pity the third cousin, Tivona Gilje, a decade older than her siblings, was no longer alive: in the online image of Nils, she was identified as the knitter of the sweater the boy had been wearing at death, a connection which implied reasonably close interaction with Nils and his parents. But she had two surviving children, the elder of whom might just have been old enough to have formed an opinion on the extended family dynamics.

Was she reading too much into this aspect of the background information surrounding the boy's death? Very possibly: it was essentially the sole solid detail they had to date, but this fact didn't make it crucial. There were seven or eight other bodies down there, of whom her team knew nothing useful at this point; any one of them might be the key to explaining exactly what had occurred here. Perhaps the boy was merely a harbinger: a gruesome grave marker, but otherwise incidental and of no broader relevance beyond the particular tragedy of a young death.

There was also the problem of Mashaka O'Meeghan. While it was clear that he could not remain directly involved in the investigation, especially while Nils was its sole identifiable focus, it would be a blow to lose his field expertise. It had been partly with this in mind that she had agreed not to inform Sabatier of O'Meeghan's apparent conflict of interest until the start of the Commander's next duty cycle: no need to disturb their supervisor's sleep, morning would be soon enough. It was an arrangement which left O'Meeghan a few precious hours in which to gain visual access to the building's annexe, and to set the UAV overflying the other nearby gullies, in search of the midden which he reasoned must be nearby.

She realised that she could use Adewale's timing of the event to develop a shortlist of potential identities of the other bodies in the ice. It was reasonable to assume they'd all met their ends at the same approximate time; so the candidates were those who had gone missing about (say) sixty to fifty-seven years ago, and had remained undiscovered in the intervening years. From Hunten, and on the list which Ngata and Whiteneck were checking, there were only two within the indicated time window, Nils himself and his mother Becki Grissom; in the other direction, from the much smaller settlement of Owen, there was one, Vid Berkowitz, a biochemist who had been just twenty-five years old at the time of his last known sighting, almost a year before Nils'. If there was any connection between Berkowitz and Grissom, or Berkowitz and Nils O'Meeghan, other than the mere fact of their disappearances from society within a year of each other, Braun couldn't discern it from a simple search. But even if there were some undiscovered link, even if Berkowitz and Grissom were among the ice-buried remains in the gully, that still left five, potentially six, bodies about whom nothing could yet be guessed, unless Prabha widened the search's geographic parameter to encompass the full farside hemisphere. She did so now, and one name—more precisely, one surname—very rapidly snagged her attention.

It might be coincidence, nothing more. People sometimes had the same last name yet were unrelated. But this was rare on Titan, with a population much smaller than Mars, smaller than many of the nations of Earth. If people shared a name, that was probably not all that connected them.

She stared ahead of herself for several seconds, then sealed off the slate and stood up. She'd scarcely done so when the slate reactivated itself, announcing an urgent call. Sabatier had started her duty cycle early, it seemed. Prabha sought to recall the form of words she had mentally prepared for the task of reporting why it had now become necessary to pause Mashaka's role in the investigation.

But Jamari Sabatier was calling about something else; and Prabha quickly realised that the case had now turned more serious, and more deadly.

NINE

The retraction had been delayed in reaching them. That was the problem.

If the retraction had been livecast to Saturn system, or to the data hubs orbiting Titan, as had been the original study which had promised so much, then they would've known the project was nonviable. But the retraction had been bumped from the feed, or perhaps had never been considered for inclusion in competition with the bandwidth-heavy entertainment and sport and news items which made up the bitwise bulk of the interplanetary signals arriving from in-system. Instead, they'd had to wait more than a year for the minuscule data parcel, shipped solid-state alongside a myriad other deprioritised items of information, Earth's back pages, arriving on an ore freighter from the Trojans. Because the Trojans had held the information, too, had apparently received it livecast from Earth, where Saturn system had not. It was how it worked. Some information was deemed sufficiently valuable to ship as light, crossing within hours from inner to outer system; some moved hostage to the sluggardly constraints of reaction mass. One could blame the custodians, the comptrollers, the schedulers, but it served no purpose to do so: the information moved as it would, and as it always had. The movement, the delay in movement, of a particular portion of data between worlds, was very seldom life-critical, and probably those who'd decided to hold back the journal issue containing the retraction had seen no reason that that decision would be any different in effect. The popular shows, the stuff which went out everywhere, or near enough everywhere, in real time, or near enough real time: those feeds were what held sway, were what most people most urgently wanted to hear from Earth. Most people.

So they'd gone ahead, at the clinic, with the technique which had held so much promise. The detail, the kernel, of that promise's falsity: that had been held in-system, had not reached them in time. If anything, it devalued itself as the months progressed, for it was old information now, and what worth did that have? But none of them in the outer system knew this, while all the while the detail lay idle in a freight ship's data hold, as good as sleeping.

And so what had happened had happened, and it was necessary to tidy things away, to remove all traces.

TEN

They had been impressively methodical.

They'd left a mess, whoever they were. Her bedroom, the mealroom, the lounge, the storage room: in each of them it seemed as though everything which could be moved had been, everything which could be overturned had been, everything which could be tipped out of its container had been dumped on the floor or on whatever bare surface was closest to hand. The bedroom was the worst, her clothing strewn wide, the bed stripped, each drawer in her bureau pulled open as far as possible, and all emptied, mundane and embarrassingly personal items, the lot of it. The bathroom too: the cabinet's contents had been swept onto the bare warmed-polymer flooring: medicinals, soaps, sanitary items and all the rest. Behind the fright of it, finding her own private space ravaged like this, there was the shame, as though somehow she had invited this herself; behind the shame of it, there was the anger. Whoever had done this had claimed a right they didn't have.

Behind the anger of it: what? The shock, the affront, the lack of connection to her normal existence.

Behind the affront, the determination to redress whatever had happened here, however that might be effected.

First she sought to learn whether anything had been stolen; though she knew with near-certainty, from the start, that it had not. This had been a hunt, not a raid. Whoever had done this, they weren't thieves.

Recognisable items of real value had held no interest for them in their search of her belongings.

It occurred to her, as she commenced putting things right, that she was disrupting a crime scene: there might be evidence of the intruders' identities which she was obliterating as she tidied. (Why did she think there'd been more than one? She'd no idea, but it made sense nonetheless. Whoever had been here had worked quickly and thoroughly, and speed and thoroughness were both easier with two, or more than two, than with one.) But though it was surely a matter on which the pol should be called, she could not involve them: it would mean further disruption, further invasion of her private space. She wanted to restore order as soon as she could; though she knew the chaos would remain, remembered, imaged. She tried to calculate whether she could sort it all in the coming days, in the time available between work and sleep and a minimum three-day trip to Hunten, before Nik was next home from Sunder's in a week's time.

Nik's room: had they trashed that too? (And what did it say about her, that she only thought this now?) But Nik's disarray was exactly as he had left it this morning; it had not been disturbed.

That, oddly, was a comfort: whatever this was about—and really, there could scarcely be any doubt—it did not concern her son, only herself.

There was something she would need to do tomorrow, early, before she commenced work.

She wondered what time Kim N'Diaye was starting these days.

ELEVEN

Siamese cats, corgis, beagles, angora rabbits, kākāpō, dunnarts... there were few nonhuman vertebrate species present on Titan, for those who felt the need of animal companionship and who wished for a pet more interactive (and perhaps more challenging of upkeep) than the several varieties of tropical and freshwater fish which populated the aquaria to be found—according to the most recent global census—in slightly more than four percent of Titan's settlements. The total number of family groups hosting one or more quadrupeds or flightless parrots was apparently only a fifth as large: for many households, even where the interest existed in doing so, it was often not affordable to provide, for such creatures, a sufficiently expansive in-home habitat to meet the standards set by animal welfare legislation. The view was common, too, that there was something unseemly or unethical in keeping as a pet some small terrestrial creature which had evolved for life on a far warmer and weightier world. With the fish, neutrally buoyant (or nearly so) within their aquaria, it was easier to argue a justification, less convincing to argue cruelty. Those who kept animals, of course, argued conversely: humans had always lived within an ecosystem alongside numerous other animals as well as plants, fungi and microorganisms; on Titan such an ecosystem was necessarily an entirely artificial construct, but such a construct did not need to aspire to minimalism, life was richer where it was more plentiful, thus it benefitted society that people kept and cared for pets.

It was an argument, a debate, which had been ongoing since humans first arrived to live on Titan, and would very likely remain so in perpetuity; and who was to say which viewpoint was correct?

In Hunten it was meerkats; that is, meerkats were not the only animals kept as pets within that settlement, nor was this the sole settlement on Titan to have a nonzero population of the small mongooses, but Hunten was the only place on Titan where there could be found, thanks to the escape of a breeding pair almost two decades earlier, meerkats living in a very rough approximation of the wild. That ancestral breeding pair had colonised a rocky corner of Hunten's small and somewhat unconvincing central park, had resisted the derisorily publicised dislodgement efforts of the authorities who, it has to be said, often had little if any experience in animal handling; and after an impressively well-organised public campaign, the escapees had been granted protected status and a guarantee that there would be no more official attempts at eviction. Regulations were passed to ensure, for the animals, access to a waterhole and the continuity of a suitable food supply—necessarily synthetic, but tailored to the meerkats' dietary requirements and preferences. Over time, the colony was augmented by the accidental or intentional release of several further individuals; a group of enthusiasts received a grant to construct several animatronic 'predators' which would mimic hazards encountered in the wild, while not posing any genuine danger to the colony's constituents—a project subsequently abandoned after repeated acts of vandalism to the robots; a unit at the University of Hunten was established to monitor (and to maintain, using gene therapy when needed) the colony's continuing genetic fitness against the risks of inbreeding; and it became commonplace for the parents of preteen children to take those offspring, on occasion, to the park, for a picnic and to view the meerkats. It was just such a family group which had discovered the body—the human body, lest there otherwise be any ambiguity—of an adult male who had met a bloody end not five metres from the meerkat warren's front entrance.

What the meerkats thought, exactly, of the numerous Hunten pol officers who were quickly on the scene cannot of course be discerned; but one can readily imagine that they were not best pleased at the intrusion and the fuss.

The briefing room table appeared longer than was materially possible within the room's confines, but then the extension wasn't a material thing; rather, it was the result of a holo connection with Hunten central pol. Braun, Adewale and O'Meeghan were joined by eight others from the Hunten force, most of whom likely knew considerably more, at this juncture, of the matter under discussion than did Prabha and her two hab-mates.

Sabatier provided a terse overview. They had found Aldous Fischetti, the young man who'd been Fil Bayley's companion on that fateful skidbike ride from Owen. They had had a good many questions to ask Fischetti, about his abandonment of Bayley and about his prior knowledge of a traversable skidbike trail connecting Owen and Hunten, not marked on any map; but he wouldn't be able to answer their queries, not now and not into the future. Braun wondered at that: had someone required Fischetti's silence?

But why mount a defence of a fifty-eight-years-old crime?

One after another, on Sabatier's direction, various of the personnel arrayed around the Hunten end of the table reported on what they'd learned in the few hours following the discovery of Fischetti's meerkat-nibbled body. Whiteneck, one of the first officers to attend the scene, described what they had encountered. He appeared ill at ease as he spoke, which was, Braun reflected, a fully understandable reaction: this might well be the first homicide victim the young officer had encountered in his career, and the accompanying visual evidence was confronting, even through holo.

'We're sure it's Fischetti?' Sabatier asked. The question would be to some extent theatrical, Prabha realised; the Inspector would already have the answer on that, but would be asking to ensure all the others had the full available information. There was also the aspect that every investigation was, to some extent, a training exercise: Brock Whiteneck would emerge from this more fully aware of effective pol conduct in these situations. That, and trauma counselling, might be the two key outcomes for him from this.

'Can confirm,' said Ryba Ngata, Whiteneck's partner and mentor, a senior officer who'd seemingly tired of looking for further career advancement. 'Holovisage on the victim's skidbike licence, found on his person. The attacker or attackers could have straightforwardly removed that, but they didn't; which may mean they wanted his identity known from the outset. We've informed the mother, one Moina Doak, just a half hour ago: distraught, obviously, poor woman, but there was something else there as well. I'd call it accusatory.'

'Accusatory?' asked Sabatier.

'Yes,' replied Ngata. 'Said this was our doing, that we'd as good as signed his death warrant by looking to bring him in for questioning last week. Brock assured her that was just routine, that her son wasn't suspected of anything; she replied that 'they' wouldn't have seen it that way.'

'And did she say who 'they' were?'

'No. Said she wasn't going to do our work for us. Doak said he'd been clean for two years, maybe longer, that we'd put a target on her son's back, and then she told us to get out. Which, the tragic news having been delivered, is what we did.'

'What do we have on Fischetti's past? It seems she's implying we should have something.'

'Nothing conclusive and nothing direct. He'd been living and working in Owen for several years, moved back here to Hunten only about ten months ago. So by the timeline suggested by the mother, we would likely have no indication of anything untoward, unless we'd requested his details from Owen pol. Which we had no reason to: he wasn't suspected of anything, in an official sense he's still not suspected of anything, he is—was—simply a witness.'

'A witness who went missing a week or more ago. He might have been abducted, but I think it more likely he was just in hiding. He could well have realised he'd be in danger, after talking to us, if there was something significantly untoward in his history.'

'You're thinking pharmhands?' Whiteneck interjected.

'Wouldn't surprise me,' replied Ngata. 'But I'm not thinking anything in particular, we don't have enough info yet.'

'Fair enough,' said Sabatier. 'The mother, Moina Doak. Do you think she knows more than she's told?'

'Possibly,' said Ngata. 'That is to say, it's obvious she knows something about hazardous and possibly nefarious past behaviour on his part. Whether it's substantive enough to help us, who knows?'

'Should we bring her in?' asked Whiteneck.

'I'd recommend we give her time,' said Ngata. 'She's distressed, rightly so, and she sees us as complicit in her son's death. Which, from her perspective, I'd say was a justifiable attitude, or at least fully understandable. It would be both counterproductive and, frankly, cruel, to push further on that right now. She's lost a son; give her time to grieve. We can check up on her in the coming weeks; she may be more forthcoming then, or she might approach us of her own accord.'

'Might she be in any danger herself?' Prabha asked.

'Possibly,' said Ngata. 'Her son had moved back home: if he was a target, she could be too.'

'We'll put her under obs,' said Sabatier. 'Discreet, of course. Ryba, I'll leave that for you to organise. Seventy-two hours, then we'll review. Hoekstra, what do we have from Pathology?'

The senior pathologist confirmed that the death had occurred as a result of blood loss following repeated stab wounds to the torso and thighs. 'Deep wounds. No sign of hesitation. Substantial tissue and organ damage,' said the pathologist, sounding almost impressed.

'Do we have the murder weapon yet?' asked Sabatier.

'No,' replied Ngata. 'Uniform are searching for it now.'

'What should they be looking for?'

'Straight blade, length of at least twenty centimetres,' said the pathologist. 'Broad point, at least two centimetres across, but the cutting edge extremely sharp at the tip, less so elsewhere. There's no indication multiple weapons were used, and in my opinion it's unlikely to be a metal blade, nor anything standard. My suspicion is it would have been home-printed. As near to untrackable as you could wish, unless the assailant were foolish enough to use a public printing facility, which seems improbable.'

'So until or unless we find it, it's probably not going to be of any use to us. That is, unless it has passed through several hands, leaving a trail we can trace.'

'Precisely,' said Hoekstra. 'My suspicion is that it's the only weapon used, wielded by just one assailant. There's an almost pleasing consistency to the wounds; multiple attackers would yield more variety.'

'One assailant. That would make it more difficult to overpower a victim, particularly one whose appearance would suggest a reasonable ability to fight back. Any defensive wounds to the hands or forearms?'

'Nothing suggesting close-quarters combat at knifepoint. Some bruising of the upper arms, consistent with being grappled from behind. I surmise this likely occurred some time before the stabbing.'

'Before? Why not during? One attacker to hold him immobilised, one to wield the weapon.'

'The bruising is very close to several of the blade wounds. Anyone holding him for that would have been placing their fingers in mortal jeopardy. I mean, I can check carefully for any blood spatter not matching Fischetti's, if you think it's worthwhile, but I don't think—'

'Let's not rule anything out,' said Sabatier.

'Very well,' replied Hoekstra. 'Which brings us to the toxicology.'

The pathologist reported that, according to the interim bloodwork, Fischetti had been drugged with what he termed a 'suggestibility cocktail'—a truth serum, in plainer language—as well as an immobilising agent; he'd then been killed. Probably the drugging had happened elsewhere, but the slaying appeared to have occurred within the park, most likely under the cover of the artificial night which was imposed to conform with the meerkats' diurnal expectations.

Then it was Prabha's turn. She described what they knew so far, eliding, at Sabatier's prior suggestion, the boy's identity; it simplified Sabatier's decision—which had quite surprised Braun, and apparently O'Meeghan himself—that she would not exclude an experienced officer from the investigation until the boy's identification was irrefutable, or until it otherwise became unavoidable. Accordingly, Prabha now reported that they had an identification of the long-dead child, but a tentative one; she described also the discovery of several further bodies, as yet unretrieved and unidentifiable. 'Here's where it gets interesting,' she told them. 'If we do get to interview Fischetti's mother, this'—she consulted the notes on her slate—'Moina Doak, we should ask her about routes between Hunten and Owen.'

'Why would she know anything about that?' asked Ngata. 'We've already established the victim has lived in both localities, several years in each; he likely could have found the route himself, just on his travels between the one and the other.'

'Perhaps,' said Braun. 'But there's another possibility. The child's remains are tentatively fifty-eight years old, closer to fifty-nine in fact, and there are several more bodies. Which means we are looking at several further people who went missing at broadly the same time. The child's mother is a possibility as one of the other bodies, though for now that's just speculative. The Hunten-Owen catchment doesn't have that many candidates within a realistic timeframe; expand it to a whole-of-Titan search, and there are dozens. Too many. But if we concentrate on a regional search for missing persons last seen between sixty and fifty-seven years ago, taking in also Woltjer, Herschel and Sola to the east, Sinton, Ponnamperuna and Rieke to the north; Huygens, Strobel and Hevelius south and/or west—that is to say, every significant settlement within about twenty-five hundred kilometres of the site, then we get eleven missing who could conceivably be considered the most likely to find within that ice, in a location not now identified, somehow, on any extant map. And one of those eleven, last seen fifty-nine years ago and never since, is Doak's father, Aldous Fischetti's grandfather, a Dr Sigbjorn Fischetti. It's purely hypothetical, but—'

'But it's worth investigating, yes,' said Sabatier.

Braun had the hab to herself. Mashaka O'Meeghan had suited up again, and had gone to see for himself the next gully past the abandoned structure, which the UAV footage showed as possessing an extended belt of nearly flattened ice: he saw this as evidence of the second frozen dump he'd been seeking. Braun was keeping an open mind: yes, this site was closer to the structure than was the mass grave, which made sense if the building's occupants had been looking to dispose of heavier furniture and machinery as well as bodies; but it might be anything, really. They'd need a decent series of tomography runs to establish whether the ice held any foreign objects of potential interest, and such a scan would take time.

Kordell Adewale had accompanied O'Meeghan out as far as the emptied building. Her goal was to set up a remote data link with Bayley's damaged skidbike: once established, this would allow her, from the comfort of her workstation, to plumb the bike's stored details of the moments preceding the collision with the boy's remains. Prabha wasn't sure what, if anything, Adewale expected to learn from the footage—Bayley's description of the incident had been fairly thorough—but she trusted her colleague's judgment on such matters. If Kordell saw value in painstaking analysis of the bike's locational metadata, then there was a point to it, and it might even yield something useful.

And Braun herself? She was just trying to make sense of it all: the structure, the unmarked route, the bodies in the ice; and now Fischetti junior's murder, and Fischetti senior's disappearance, all those years past. Did they connect, and if so, how?

Fischetti's murder was the most immediate, and thus the most pressing.

The immobilising agent suggested that Aldous Fischetti had been fully aware, but powerless to react physically to an execution which had not prioritised speed. Braun flinched as her mind role-played it. She very much hoped that that detail had not been conveyed to the victim's mother. Surely, though, Ngata was sufficiently experienced to have reported only the crucial aspects: her son's death; the absence, as yet, of any witnesses to the crime; the—

She leaned forward, crafted a short message to Sabatier: *meerkat cams?* Almost certainly, someone on the scene in Hunten had already considered this aspect; but it never hurt to check. And while it was unlikely that the feeds of meerkat behaviour would show anything of great value to the investigation, unlikely wasn't impossible. If nothing else, it might allow them to refine the timing of the crime, which would simplify the task of seeking to unravel the assailant's movements before or after.

It was a brutal way to die: fully aware, most likely, yet unable to self-defend. The implied sequence of events was theatrical, was very clearly intended to send a message. But to whom was it directed, and who had sent it on its way?

Adewale and O'Meeghan were back sooner than expected, and in a state of something approaching excitement. Braun waited for them to enter the airlock, but they didn't. Instead, Kordell Adewale's voice buzzed at her from her slate. 'We need the drill. I've persuaded Mashaka that he needs to drill a hole in the derelict's floor.'

'Persuaded is perhaps overstating it,' said O'Meeghan. 'I told her there's no virtue in breaking a perfectly good drill bit purely on spec. But she explained it, and she does have a point.'

'Explained what?' Prabha asked.

'The terrain around the structure isn't perfectly level,' said Adewale. 'But the structure itself has a flat floor, where in some places they would have needed to dig down maybe twenty centimetres, maybe further, to achieve a level surface for construction. That's a lot of effort, for no apparent benefit. It would have been simpler and quicker, and better from a heat-engineering perspective to build on the existing terrain, establish a foundation, and sit the structure on top of that. So why would they not go for the easy option? It implies that digging in had some benefit for them.'

'I don't see where you're going with this.'

'The drill set is in a lockbox in O'Meeghan's room, the red one. Just bring it and suit up.'

'Suit up?' asked Prabha.

'We'll need some help with the IPR rig. It's going to be cumbersome to manoeuvre it through the building.'

'Why would we want to do that?'

'I don't think the building is single-storey.'

Seven hours later, she placed a call to Sabatier. 'We'll need reinforcements,' she told her supervisor, not caring about the lateness of the hour according to Sabatier's schedule, not even bothering with any opening pleasantries. 'And I'll need transport home—I've been away from Lassa long enough, and there's way too much still to explore here.'

'Fair enough,' said Jamali Sabatier. 'Though I'd appreciate a bit more context here.'

Prabha gave her the context, then went to pack.

TWELVE

It was good to see Neve again, of course. Guerline felt compelled to mentally add the 'of course', for reasons she couldn't properly describe to herself.

It must have been a year or so, it was more than a year since she'd last seen Neve, when she had last visited Woltjer for her mother's seventieth. Back then it had still been Neve-and-Thanh, which perhaps it still was or perhaps not; but in any case it was a little odd to now be meeting just the one and not the pair. It was odder still to hear Neve speak in her own reconstructed voice, after the years of self-imposed silence. Perhaps what was oddest had been the timing of Neve's message, which had followed so close, less than five minutes, after an abruptly terminated enquiry to Runag Fischetti. Scarfe at first thought the two communications—her calls to Runag and from Neve—to have been connected; but apparently not.

Guerline had insisted that they dine at Miriam's, a newish outer-system fusion restaurant on the edge of Trafton's fashionable northern dining precinct. It was a small establishment, crowded and with little if any thought devoted to aesthetics, but she confidently expected that her dinner guest would be won over by the cuisine.

Neve was well. Guerline found her gaze repeatedly returning to the line of scar tissue across her friend's forehead, not yet concealed by the bangs which she was apparently attempting to grow out. It was a big change, to be encountering Neve without the circlet, and without Thanh.

Guerline at first found it difficult to provide any direction to the conversation, but this was hardly a problem: Neve was happy to provide an update, unprompted. Perhaps she was making up for the years of voicelessness.

Thanh was well. Things in Woltjer were much the same. Neve had seen Guerline's mother recently, at an art event; her mother's health appeared as good as could be expected. This visit to Trafton had been necessary for work, she was hoping to catch up, also, with Kim N'Diaye during the two-day visit. No, it was generous of Guerline to offer, but she'd had accommodation booked and paid for several weeks in advance, close to the installation she'd be working on.

'What about—,' Guerline began, and then reflected that it wasn't really appropriate to be redirecting the conversation along those lines, for all that she had been both puzzled and hurt by Runag's brusque, even angry response when Guerline had tried calling earlier. Neve was Woltjer-based these days, and busy in the art scene there, while Runag was in Sagan working, if Guerline recalled correctly, as a T-suit-insurance underwriter; for all she knew the pair had even less contact now than did she with either of them. Instead she said simply 'So how are things really?', as though this was not information which Neve had been divulging, for the last ten minutes or so, entirely off her own bat.

But it's true that sometimes the stupidest questions get the deepest responses. 'We are still feeling our way,' said Neve, slowly and after several seconds. 'I think in some respects it's been easier for me than for Thanh— in my case, it has just been a matter of unlearning my need to view him as a conduit for all verbal interaction with the wider world, whereas he has had more of a juggle, if that makes sense, in rebalancing between thought and spoken word. I think that was always something more difficult for him than for me, we both had to learn, before, to shield our private thoughts to ensure they weren't picked up and conveyed by the gear; I fancy I was a quick learner at that and, well, he got there too, but there are still things about the way he thinks which I didn't need to know, don't need to know; not bad things, but— distracting, I think I will leave it at that.

If you want more you'll have to order more wine, I'm not paying for my own self-incrimination. Or for his.'

'It's good to hear you again,' said Guerline, acknowledging to herself that this was true; acknowledging also that she could weep a little too, in reaction to the changing circumstances, but she chose not to. It had been a while since she'd last seen Neve; it had been far longer since she'd properly heard her, since anyone, probably, had properly heard her, or anyone other than Thanh. There was a part of Guerline's reaction—and this might be something she could never divulge—which was hesitant about endorsing this change in Neve's mode of interaction with the world, because the previous mode had required, she could see now, such bravery on Neve's part as well as on Thanh's. But it really was no business of hers how anybody else chose to live, so long as harm wasn't done; and neither Neve nor Thanh was anybody's project.

It was neither necessary nor helpful to view everyone as she viewed her clients; it was just that sometimes, with some people in particular, it was a difficult instinct to avoid.

Neve broke the silence before it could grow too durable. 'I almost forgot, I brought something for Niki.' She reached into her bag and pulled out a cellulose-boxed toy icemover, a blade-fronted half-track in an improbably metallic blue.

'Thank you,' said Guerline, inspecting the toy briefly—she suspected he already had this one, though not in this colour—before placing it carefully in her own bag.

'He's still collecting the vehicles, yes?'

'More or less,' said Guerline, surprising herself by the lack of enthusiasm in her voice. Neve, too, picked up on it, asked if Niki was perhaps outgrowing such things.

'Not exactly,' said Guerline. 'Or at least not yet. But.'

'But?'

She told Neve about the kite, and the effusiveness, not to say the insistence, with which Nik spoke about kiting, and about his readiness for a lock licence. Neve replied that this was only to be encouraged;

and there it was, the unspoken tension always present, under the surface, the danger beneath the ice on which she and Neve met: for Neve was outdoorsy, insofar as this was possible for anyone on Titan, or at least anyone who dwelt in a large and urbanised settlement, to be outdoorsy, as Freyne, Guerline's brother had been, and as Guerline herself was not, though she'd sought for a couple of years to be so, or to at least pretend to be so, for a couple of years; and then the accident which had taken Neve's voice and Freyne's life, those eight or nine years ago, after Guerline had stopped pretending, after Nikita had arrived. And now Guerline and Neve were on opposite sides of the question of a lock licence for a child too young to remember his uncle, an uncle—brother to one, and close friend or lover to the other—who was ultimately the reason these two women knew each other, the reason they maintained a connection. So now Guerline merely nodded as though in agreement with what the other was saying; nodded and held her tongue.

She busied herself with the next small platter's offerings. They had ordered the banquet, which was excellent and varied but which offered just a little too much of everything; now it was a stack of small drumsticks, irregular knobs of synthetic meat on grown bone, coated in a fragrant and hyper-sticky glaze which promised to be sweet but which was instead strongly and somehow sharply savoury.

Evidently the drumsticks met with Neve's approval also. 'These are the best yet,' she said. 'Really, they could have just brought out a bigger platter with more of only this, and we wouldn't have needed all the rest. I mean it was good too, all of it's been good, but—'

'But then you would have missed the dip. It's up next, or possibly the course after that one. Make sure you leave some space for that. Trust me, the dip is what brings people back here.'

'Not this one? I would've thought—'

Guerline's slate chimed. *Sunder*, she thought to herself. *Or maybe Toan, if there's been something come up at work. Or Fil, or at an outside chance, Prabha Braun.* But when she checked, which she had felt she needed to, it wasn't any of those. 'I'm going to have to take this.

I'll be right back,' she told Neve, then got up and made her way to the restaurant's rear. She hoped none of the other patrons were going to need the restroom for the next few minutes.

It was more than a quarter hour before she was able to rejoin Neve at the small table. The fabled dip had been and gone. 'I did try to save you some,' said Neve. 'That at least was the plan; I'm not quite sure what happened.'

Guerline smiled, determined not to put a damper on the evening, despite the slate call's import. But perhaps Neve read something on her face, because she stood up. 'It has been great catching up,' she told Scarfe. 'But now I must get some shut-eye, or tomorrow won't go well.'

Guerline stood again, and they hugged. This too was a new development; Neve had never been one for hugging. Perhaps, Guerline mused, it was sensory compensation for the absence of the thought-sharing which her friend had practised with Thanh for the past several years.

But, as with so many things, it was not really any of her business; and not everybody was a client.

Back home, she could not settle. The conversation with Kim N'Diaye just ran on a track, a circular track, within her mind, embarking again immediately upon reaching its destination.

She had been furious at first, explaining that she had given Kim the vial purely for safekeeping, because it clearly hadn't been safe in her own possession—had she not made that clear to him? She was sure she had.

Evidently she had not. Kim for his part had been apologetic; and he was never so eloquent, nor so mellifluous, as when dealing with sensitive subjects. 'I am sorry,' is what his reply had amounted to, when it boiled down; and he'd sounded it. 'I misinterpreted, assumed you were asking for an analysis of the residue.'

'If I was asking for an analysis of the residue,' said Guerline, 'I would have asked for an analysis of the residue.'

'I joined the dots,' said Kim. 'My apologies that they weren't mine to join.'

'It's done now,' Guerline had responded, sighing. 'I'll collect the vial in the morning.'

'I don't think I can accommodate that. This will need to go to the pol.'

'That's who I'm taking it to.'

'Then I can save you the bother.'

'The Hunten pol, not the Trafton pol. It's their vial. Not that they exactly know that yet.'

'How did it come to be in your possession?'

'I'm not at liberty to divulge that. Is there enough material left for them to analyse?'

'Probably not. There wasn't much to begin with, and Gab Laycock needed most of what was there, to be sure of what we were dealing with.'

'And what are we dealing with?'

'I'm not at liberty to divulge that.' (She'd been able to hear the grin, then, as he echoed her words back to her.) 'Guerline, really, the best approach is to take this directly to the pol, the Trafton pol, and they can pass it on to Hunten. I can take it myself.'

'I can't let you. Look, Kim, I need to travel to Hunten tomorrow evening, with… a client, and the vial is part of h— of their testimony. An important part. Plus it will probably fall to me to explain how it was inadvertently analysed, which will be more straightforward for all concerned if it's back in my possession for that. Please?'

'And I suppose you're going to require the results of that inadvertent analysis to pass on to them…'

'That would be very helpful, with most of the residue gone.'

'Fine. Don't ask me why, but it was never officially logged, probably because it was never officially onboarded; Gab just had time on her hands this afternoon, so she ran it through. It's an illegal drug.'

'A narcotic?'

'No.'

'Well, then what?'

She'd heard Kim's sigh loud and clear, even against the restaurant's background noise. 'It would be really useful to know the provenance on this,' he'd said, 'given that this has Sigbjorn Fischetti's name printed on the vial label as the authorising physician.'

'It goes without saying—that is, I hope it does—that word of this shouldn't reach Runag's ears.'

'Of course. I'm not so foolish as to mention this sort of thing to her.'

Was that a dig? Guerline wondered.

'There's another name too,' said Kim. 'In the administering physician's field. Rather, it should be a name; it's just a number. 54, whatever that might mean.'

'I've no idea,' said Guerline. 'All I can say, really, is that it was found within Hunten's jurisdiction, and is surmised not to be recent.'

'Found by your client?'

'I can't divulge. Kim, what are we— what is Hunten pol dealing with here?'

There was another sigh; but then he did tell her. It had taken him a few minutes to properly explain.

And then she'd emerged, stony-faced, from the restroom, and had made her way back to Neve's table.

She lay in bed, waiting for sleep to find her, knowing it would likely take a while.

That poor kid, she thought, picturing the skidbike collision which had precipitated all this. *I wonder what they thought was wrong with him.*

THIRTEEN

Braun was done with the site: there was nothing she could contribute out here that she couldn't also do, and likely more effectively, back in Hunten. Adewale was still poring through the skidbike's data—though really, what could that tell them that they didn't already know?—and O'Meeghan was continuing with the lidar and IPR mapping of the ice midden. Both were tasks with which she couldn't usefully assist. She'd participated in the search of the gutted structure, a search which had unearthed Bayley's damaged skidbike; that was where her meaningful involvement had, in effect, ended. Someone else could take on the exploration of the structure's blocked-off basement, once they'd established a means of access to it.

But Sabatier wasn't ready, yet, to facilitate Prabha's return to Hunten. Something about personnel constraints in regard to the ongoing investigation; as though the pilots were also all fully occupied in the search for Aldous Fischetti's killer or killers. But perhaps they were.

There was her daughter too, of course. This didn't mark the first time, since Prabha's return to work five months after Lassa's birth, that she had needed to be away from her child for more than a daycycle, but it was already easily the longest such stint and would be easily longer still, in view of the required round-trip time, whenever she did return. Not that she had significant concerns regarding Lassa's wellbeing and socialisation: her housemate (and de facto mother-in-law) cared deeply for, and was well trusted by, her grandchild. Prabha suspected some people considered

it strange that she had chosen to cohabit with the mother of the man
she'd chosen not to, rather than with her own mother and her mother's
partner, but it was a domestic arrangement that worked to everyone's
advantage, including the child's: Braun's mother's life was too busy for
frequent contact with a small child, her mother-in-law's life was not.
It was simply necessary to avoid discussion of certain topics, chief among
those being the life and death of Lassa's father, Laszlo Trolove; but this
avoidance seemed to occur naturally, nowadays, by mutual assent.

'Got something,' Adewale said, pushing into the briefing room with a
fully expanded slate. She took a seat beside Prabha, who looked up from
the latest Hunten-sent summary.

'What?'

'You need to see it.'

'You know I can't read those numbers,' Prabha cajoled.

'This is footage. One of the features of the Xu Powerglide is that it
piggybacks on the operator's T-suit's HUD. So we get to see what Fil
Bayley saw, leading up to the collision. And beyond. The feed can be
deleted or archived, but by default the most recent one hundred and
twenty minutes of operation is retained. Bayley opted to delete it; but the
deletion is only of the data pointers, the registry values, not the footage
files themselves. It was quite straightforward to find. And the question
is—or one of the questions is—why would she do that?'

'Yes, that's a pertinent question,' said Prabha. 'So she deleted the
HUD view? I guess that's understandable, though — it must have been
a quite horrific encounter, she wouldn't want to be reminded of it every
time she donned her T-suit.'

'We don't know about the HUD data within the T-suit, though; that's
not something we chose to pursue, apparently, when we arranged that
interview with Scarfe accompanying her. No, I'm talking only about
the bike's copy of that HUD data. Bayley had the presence of mind to
select file deletion, after she apparently became aware she had left the

piggybacking in place, substantially after the collision with the frozen boy.'

'I don't follow.'

'It's best if you see the footage.'

'I've no interest in watching the collision.'

'No, and I don't blame you. But this isn't that. It's from when she had finished dragging the bike to the structure.' She angled the slate's screen more directly towards Braun, intoned: 'Play, half-speed with steadying, timepoint six to timepoint seven, hold on final image.'

The vid was low-light grainy, less informative to begin with than the accompanying audio, which Prabha surmised was the slowed recording of Bayley's grunts and imprecations as she dragged something behind her. 'Is there any particular context to this segment of the record?' Braun asked.

'It's post-collision, and after several other sequences: Bayley has picked herself up, Fischetti approaches her, checks that her suit's intact, that she's not badly damaged, they establish that the Xu is a write-off—and get this, then he more or less chastises her for not having brought a replacement front skid, as though that's a thing people do when biking, as though that would actually have allowed them to effect a field repair to it—and then he says he needs to be back in Hunten, and she has oxygen replenishment for days and she can just walk to the Kuiper-Hunten trackway a few kilometres north, and he leaves. I don't wish to speak ill of the dead, but. There's about ten minutes of her swearing after that, without much repetition, which is impressive in itself in someone of such tender years; and then she walks off for a bit: not in the trackway's direction, but back the way they had been travelling. The piggybacking falls out for a couple of minutes, her suit's out of the bike's range; when it reestablishes, her breathing's very rapid and the med signals are pretty much standard early-onset stress responses.'

'She's seen the remains.'

'That seems almost certain, yes. Then for a couple of minutes she doesn't seem to know where to look, or what to do, her breathing stays rushed and then ebbs; my guess is the suit's life support has taken the summary decision to tranquilise her; anyway, the med signals stabilise after several minutes. She turns the T-suit's headlamps on for a few seconds, then douses them, then she looks in the direction of the abandoned structure, starts towards it, returns after about ten seconds to grab the bike, then she starts dragging it with her. That's where this sequence starts from. I'll say this for her, she must be bloody fit. I wouldn't be able to drag that thing, with its skid snapped like that, and I doubt you could either.'

It was now possible to discern the structure towards which Bayley was labouring, still some distance away.

'What am I supposed to be looking out for?' Prabha asked.

'You'll know it when it happens,' said Adewale.

'Very well, but can we accelerate towards that point?'

'Step forward eight minutes real time,' Adewale instructed the slate. 'Step forward one further minute. One further thirty seconds. There.'

Bayley had reached the structure, was lodging the damaged bike in the narrow open courtyard where Prabha remembered having found it. The view shifted again as Bayley stepped back, made her way around the wall towards the airlock cavity and stopped. Then the scene dipped towards, evidently, a section of the icy ground. A small object was visible more-or-less midview: Prabha couldn't discern its nature. Bayley's gloved hand moved into the view's staging area, and when she stood up once more, the object was no longer visible. The image froze. 'She picked something up.'

'Yes.'

'She didn't mention this in the interview we had with her and Scarfe. Might it have been something which had fallen off the skidbike?'

'Conceivably. But it's not a component.'

'How can you tell?'

'Last minute before timepoint seven, half-speed, apply steadying, enhance image to one sigma confidence level. Replay, hold on at timepoint seven minus three seconds.'

'Enhance?' Prabha asked.

'It's not ideal, because it can introduce artefacts. So it wouldn't be admissible in this form. But the lighting is so low that it's necessary for clarity, for our purposes here.'

Bayley again noticed the object, bent to pick it up. This time, the image paused with the object in full view.

'A container of some kind,' said Prabha.

'A vial.'

'So why wouldn't she report this to us? It was noteworthy enough in her view to pick it up.'

'And to pocket it, and then to switch off her HUD's record retention.' Adewale folded the slate, stood up, and left Braun to her thoughts.

The route wasn't marked, so it wasn't well travelled. People didn't know it existed. But an iceway of several hundred kilometres doesn't just create itself: a work gang had marked it, levelled it, smoothed it for vehicular convenience. That took time, that took effort. It didn't make sense that the iceway had been abandoned, in the same way that the structure had been abandoned. People walked away from buildings on Titan, when upkeep became too difficult, when a location became unsafe, when it became obvious that things were not working out, one way or another. But an iceway between existing settlements would stay in use, because people would still need to travel on occasion.

Mashaka had worked out the distances. The disused Owen-Hunten route was almost ten kilometres shorter than the accepted route which arced to meet the Kuiper-Hunten trackway; it likely wasn't faster, because the surface hadn't been finished to the same standard, but there were always some who preferred to take the most direct road to any destination. They would have used the iceway, had they known about it. Why, by and large, hadn't they?

Braun had taken it on herself to inquisit this. *Someone goes to a lot of trouble to build a road, which then falls out of use. Why?*

Because someone hides it?

But how do you hide a road?

You make sure it's not shown on the maps. It might not even matter that it's shown on old maps. People don't navigate by old maps, it's not safe to do so on a world where so many simple errors can kill you. They trust new maps, because new maps show you how things are now.

But like a road, a map doesn't just call itself into existence. Someone creates it; someone builds it. Someone leaves important information off it. But do they do so by accident, or with intent?

FOURTEEN

Paschel Othman took a seat opposite Guerline's desk. Fil's mother appeared ill at ease. She had been flinty, Guerline recalled, at her previous appointment, when she'd been accompanied by her parents. Perhaps she didn't like offices, or meeting rooms; perhaps her antipathy was towards those who inhabited them.

Guerline cut to the chase. 'This is a follow-up session, mostly. But also because I wanted to seek your advice, on whether Fil might require access to additional support. In view of her friend's death.'

'Her friend's death?'

'Aldous Fischetti.'

'The boy who left her at the scene of the crash?'

He was twenty-four, Guerline commented to herself. *I'd hardly call him a 'boy'.* 'He was killed in Hunten a couple of days ago.'

'Killed? You mean deliberately?'

'Yes.'

'Are you saying Fil is in danger too?'

'I don't believe so. From what I gather, this appears to relate to Fischetti's… historical activities, from before he'd met Fil. The Hunten pol have apprehended and charged the attacker, a man from Owen with a history of violence and narcotics crime, based on surveillance footage from a wildlife enclosure. There's no apparent connection with Fil; this goes back several years on Aldous's side, and appears to be a result of misinterpretation of the pol's interest in speaking with Fischetti after Fil's incident, which itself has not been publicised because of sensitivities while the… remains await identification.'

'So why are you raising this, if it's not related to Fil?'

'It's not related to Fil, but it's connected to her by Aldous Fischetti. Someone she knew, someone she'd travelled with, has been killed. I know the pol have informed her; I need to know how she is coping with the news. And I thought it best to check with you on that, before assessing whether it would be useful for me to approach her personally, in an official capacity.'

Othman was silent for several seconds. 'She hasn't told us any of this,' she said carefully.

'It's likely she needs time to process the news.'

Othman nodded, glanced away before making what seemed to be a conscious, maybe a demanding effort to meet Scarfe's gaze. 'We're grateful for what you've done for her, of course. Please don't think we're not. And I'm grateful, too, that you're making the time to accompany her to Hunten to pick up her skidbike. I don't have the time myself to do that right now. But I don't think further contact with her, after that, is going to be useful. As connected as you've become with all of this, in her mind. No offence, but I think she just needs to move on from… this, and I don't think that's something you can help her with.'

'No offence taken,' Scarfe assured her. 'I appreciate that you must know her best. I see a lot of people in difficulties of one form or another, and you get a sense for how people are managing, what they are able to cope with. I think your daughter is going to be fine. She's been well looked after, by you and her grandparents; that much is obvious.'

'Thank you.'

'If it's required, parents—well, guardians, which includes your own parents, too, obviously—also have access to support services. So please do let me know if you would like help arranging anything of that nature, for you or your parents. I know this won't have been easy for you, for any of you.'

'Thank you.'

'It must have been a comfort having them so close at hand, for you as well as for Fil,' said Scarfe. 'With something like this happening.'

'Mostly it has been.'

'I must admit I have had some concerns about how your mother is managing with this. Am I right in inferring that she has health issues?'

'She's eighty-five years old. That's a health issue in itself.'

'Nothing further?'

'Who knows?' Paschel Othman let slip some visible exasperation. 'She won't see a doctor.'

'And yet... am I right in saying she had a career in nursing?'

'Maybe that's why she won't see a doctor. Like a tradesperson who won't do their own home repairs.'

Or a divorced reconciliator, thought Guerline. 'But she's managing okay, with the... fallout from Fil's incident?'

If Othman's responses to this point had been guarded, now the shutters came down completely. 'She's doing fine, all things considered. Ms Scarfe, I'm short of time to complete a project, so with your leave, I'm going to have to finish up now. Thank you for your concern, and for the advice you've given Fil.' She stood up to go.

Guerline pleaded a migraine as justification for finishing the afternoon at home

It wasn't strictly true, but she didn't have anything time-critical on her agenda, and there were things she needed to check.

The door chirped. Her visitor—her return visitor, if her suspicion was correct—made no effort to disguise his appearance. Checking the doorcam feed, she gave thought briefly to not answering the door, or to setting her slate to record. Instead she quickly placed the slate on the mealroom counter and instructed the device to sound an alarm tone, full volume, in three minutes if not countermanded before that time.

She bade the door open.

He strode in, forced the door closed behind him. 'This has gone far enough,' he told her, his tone claiming authority. He was clad in loose-fitting sleeveless and short-legged garments which appeared designed to show off the musculature of his limbs. Scarfe thought back to the X-rig in the Bayley-Petrakis residence as she casually appraised his fitness. Tesar Bayley was easily twice Guerline's age, or more, but he plainly had more than twice her physical strength.

'I'd ask you to sit down,' Scarfe responded, striving to keep her voice level. 'I'm sure you know where all the furniture is already, from the day before yesterday. That was you, wasn't it?'

He took a half-step towards her. 'I'm not here to play games.'

'I don't doubt that,' said Scarfe, taking a reflexive half-step back. 'But I think you'll agree this is a serious matter all around. I don't mean the breaking and entering, I see no reason to press charges over that, provided it isn't repeated. I mean the incident fifty-eight years ago, which I learnt about through the labelling on the vial, and through the remaining traces of its former contents. That was what you were looking for, night before last, wasn't it?'

Something shifted in Tesar Bayley's expression; now his age showed. 'Let me see it.'

'I can't do that right now; it's somewhere else for safekeeping. And it's crucial evidence. I'm obliged to forward it to the police.'

'Crucial? No. There are dozens of those things, once per day per patient, dumped out in the ice out there. The pol will find them all soon enough. Just not this one, not right now. Please don't do that to her.' Bayley's voice quavered.

'Don't do—' Scarfe was interrupted by a piercing note from the mealroom. 'Shit. Excuse me a moment.'

She returned to the room. If Bayley was confused at the sound which had interrupted them, he didn't show it.

'She's got two months left, if that,' Tesar Bayley told her. 'I reckon it'll take them that long to connect the dots. Just let her go knowing that I've sorted it. She deserves that. I've seen what this has done to her, these past fifty-odd years. Once she's gone, I'll turn myself in—I can handle that, and I have a share in the responsibility. For the cover-up, if not for the deaths themselves.'

'You re-drew the maps, yes?'

Tesar Bayley nodded. 'Our firm had the contract for the carto update. I made sure I was the field surveyor for that sector. It wasn't difficult. My boss knew I had a thing with one of the women, but he thought that was in Owen itself. He didn't know about the clinic's location.'

'So you did it for Liv. Falsified maps on which people rely, sometimes in circumstances which could be life or death.'

'No. I mean falsified, yes, but not for Liv. I was seeing Wei Ilhan at the time, but the reason for the cover-up was the same. They were both on the vials; they both played a part in what happened. But Wei couldn't handle the aftermath, she took a quick way out, soon after. I connected with Liv a couple of months after the funeral. She'd been stewing with it, all alone. I leant her my ear, figured she needed that. She listened to me too, when I needed that. We went from there. Was it the surveying that tipped you off?'

'No, that just confirmed my suspicions. It was the names on the vial. Authorising physician: Sigbjorn Fischetti. Administering physician: no name, just the number 54. Converted to Roman numerals, that spelled it out. The surveying connection cemented it. And when I checked it out— it's there if you search back far enough in the official records, though she's done her best to obscure it over the years—she'd worked as a nurse, in the years since, but Liv was originally trained as a doctor. That's not a career progression which makes sense otherwise.'

'She thought a lower profile would be safer.'

'She was probably right,' said Guerline. 'The rest of it I got from the residue analysis— which I didn't request, by the way, I had just decided to place the vial with a... colleague in a different profession, for safekeeping, after your escapade here the day before yesterday. So you can thank yourself for that particular piece of the puzzle pie; I wouldn't have learned it otherwise. Athermolidizine dihydrochloride, briefly hailed as the first genuinely effective cryoprotectant compound, metabolically harmless and ushering in a new era of thoroughly suspended animation; identified within just a month or so as a problematic failure, effectively lethal in the doses thought necessary for true cryopreservation. No other therapeutic uses; it's not manufactured any more, because it serves no valid medicinal purpose. I don't really follow why it was being used when the problems were so well known.'

'The problems weren't known here, not until later. That information was very slow to reach Titan. So Liv thought—they all thought—the treatment was another chance at life, for people whose conditions were terminal, and currently untreatable. They were pausing them, until cures had been developed for those cancers and other conditions. There's several that are specific to Titan, caused by tholin exposure and such, things that don't happen on Earth or elsewhere. There's one, Bilpin's sarcoma, which can have a long initial dormancy but is very quick acting once it reaches the end stages, weeks usually—it's treatable now, in the early stages of malignancy at least, but back then there was nothing. Liv didn't know, none of them knew, they had no way of knowing, that the cryo prep killed the patients. It's what she has now, that sarcoma, and she could've sought treatment. But she didn't. I suppose she thought—' Bayley coughed, cleared his throat before he went on. 'So I'm asking you: please let her go. Her arrest wouldn't achieve anything; she'd be dead before she could face trial.'

Guerline was silent a few seconds. 'This clinic—it wasn't registered, was it?'

Bayley lifted his head to respond. 'Liv told me that there wasn't time. Or rather, that there had been time, of course, but Sigbjorn Fischetti was keen to get it into operation quickly. He was one of those charismatic types, overly confident, I didn't like him one bit, but that's by the by. The treatment wasn't approved, but Sigbjorn was sure the approval would be issued sooner or later, and he saw that people would be dead of this condition, and others, before the bureaucracy had ticked all the boxes. He was determined the clinic's operation was all thoroughly documented, but privately, so what they'd been doing could be legitimised after the fact. Anticipatory compliance, I think was the term he used. But the approval kept getting delayed. And then— He was one of them, one of the ones who had Bilpin's. So Liv had to dose him too.' Bayley paused as though to reconsider. 'I suppose that might better explain the regulatory impatience on his part.'

'What about the boy, the body Fil hit with the skidbike? I know she feels responsible, she feels a sense of guilt for having hit him, as though she had killed him herself, which of course she didn't. Was his condition terminal, too?'

'I—' This time Bayley's cough got caught partway, and he shook his head slightly, maybe to clear it. 'Let's just say yes,' he said. 'For Fil's sake.'

FIFTEEN

There were no direct flights from Trafton to Hunten; instead, Guerline and Fil took a five-hour flight to Woltjer on one of the new Volker electroprops, then a three-hour stopover in Woltjer air terminal before another flight, about as long as the first, to Hunten on an older, larger, and somehow more crowded craft. Scarfe had been hoping her companion would use the opportunity presented by this full day's travel for discussion or advice on how they would manage things once they reached Hunten, but Fil's slate apparently held more interest than her predicament, more interest too than her window-seat view as they swept steadily westward above Xanadu's smudged afternoon shadows, shortening as the plane outpaced the slow-setting sun.

Their luggage was checked through. The delay in Woltjer had been just long enough for time to drag—the sense that an opportunity for progress was being wasted—and just short enough that any idea of contacting her mother, or Neve and Thanh, was futile, a social duty that must wait for another time.

Scarfe had given much thought, while she was packing, about whether to include the vial in her luggage, and how to handle the question of its disclosure to the Hunten pol investigators. She still had no idea whether the decision she'd made was the right one. Perhaps there wasn't one of those.

*

Scarfe had expected Fil to take the lead in Hunten, in navigational matters at least; after all, the young woman had lived here several months, and presumably must know the byways here rather better than did Guerline, a Hunten first-timer. But Fil Bayley's reluctance to deploy her prior knowledge of the settlement was obvious, and spoke of a more general unease. So Guerline took charge; her slate probably knew its way around better than either of them.

They'd booked accommodation in a corridor hotel that advertised itself as "family-friendly, and only ten minutes' walk from the meerkats", whatever that meant. More importantly, their room for the night was less than a kilometre from the Hunten pol station, and half that, or near enough, from Braun's residence, which was to be their first port of call tomorrow morning.

It had been a long day's travel, and Scarfe was struck as always by just how exhausting was the combination of unfamiliarity and bodily near-immobility that was involved in long-distance travel. Once they had settled into the modest suite which Guerline had booked, she suggested they order food in, from the limited range of dishes on offer, rather than head out in search of a restaurant. Bayley agreed, but without anything which could be called enthusiasm; Scarfe suspected her response, had she suggested the other option, would have been the same dull acquiescence.

Guerline sought to find a conversational way between them, as they waited for the food, and then as they ate, but the effort was one-sided. Ultimately she just let Fil be: if she didn't wish to socialise, she didn't have to. Scarfe had plenty to occupy her mind, in any case.

From the shared room's other bed, Fil snored; Guerline's sleep was late arriving and of poor quality, but it would have to do.

Fil had been more animated over breakfast. Scarfe still wouldn't call her manner chatty, exactly, but it offered hope that her companion might manage to get well enough through the morning's trials. But the apprehension resurfaced as they approached the apartment, heightened as Guerline stepped into the doorbell's line of sight.

'She's got a two-year old kid,' said Scarfe, as gently as she could. 'This is just a home visit, more or less. I'm sure it'll be fine.'

'When should I tell her about the… item?'

'I'll give you a cue,' Guerline assured her. 'If it even needs to come up.'

'If?'

The door opened. Standing in the doorway was a tallish, stoutish woman of—Guerline surmised—somewhere between fifty-five and sixty-five years of age and, briefly, a small child, a girl, who quickly hid behind the woman's slacks.

'You're here to see Prabha, yes? I'm Hara, I'm Lassa's grandmother. Please come in. Prabha's just taking a call, she will be through in a minute.'

'Thank you. I'm Guerline Scarfe. And this is Fil Bayley.'

'Of course. Please come in.'

Guerline followed her down a short hallway; Fil tagged behind. The girl had run ahead, and wasn't in the small lounge which Hara led them into. 'Tea? Coffee? Water?'

'Water will be fine, thanks,' said Guerline, taking one of the indicated seats.

'Grey tea for me, if you've got it,' said Fil. 'No sweetener.'

'We know about the vial,' said Prabha, looking at Fil.

Guerline put her glass down on the shelf beside her. 'How?' she asked, before Fil had time to respond. *Has Tesar turned himself in?*

'When it became obvious that the site was… more problematic than we'd first thought, we had occasion to check the skidbike's stored data. This gave us imagery of the moments before the… collision. It also gave us vid of Ms Bayley here, outside the building, picking up a small object which had been dislodged from the ice by her bike's rear skid.'

'Am I in trouble?' Fil asked, quiet-voiced.

'The footage isn't admissible,' said Braun. 'That is to say, the imagery which is identifiable from the bike itself is within scope of the investigation, but the vid relating to the vial was cloned automatically from your suit, which is not covered by the warrants we obtained. So we know about it, but we can't officially act upon it. Nonetheless, it goes without saying that we would appreciate the vial's return—it might prove useful to our investigation.'

'This is on me,' said Scarfe. 'I didn't think to bring it.'

Braun's gaze narrowed as she renewed her focus on Guerline. 'And just how did that come to be your decision, and not Fil's?'

'It was given to me for safekeeping. Fil had shown it to her mother, who'd reacted adversely to the sight of it—'

'Why would her mother have such a reaction?'

'Because she knew something about the cover-up of what had happened there. Probably not much, but enough to be concerned at the unexpected appearance of a vial found in the vicinity.'

'And she knew this because?'

'Her father—that's Fil's grandfather, Tesar Bayley—was a part of the cover-up.'

Fil met Guerline's gaze with a stunned stare. 'What?'

'Tesar Bayley,' said Braun. 'Yes, that's a name which had already come to our attention. Can you shed any light on that involvement?'

'He was connected with one of the women at the… centre. Wei Ilhan. He edited the map so the route Fil and Aldous Fischetti later travelled on wasn't marked. He did that to protect Ilhan. This was all before he moved to Trafton, and before he got together with Fil's grandmother.'

From the look on Fil's face, the detail on her grandfather's prior relationship was new to her. From the expression on Prabha's, it wasn't.

'Wei Ilhan is also a name we'd encountered,' said Prabha.

'May I ask how?' said Guerline.

'The vial in Fil's possession, or now apparently in yours, is not the only one. There are numerous others, most of them emptied, some of them unused and still bearing their original contents, which my colleagues have removed from a… disposal site. Like yours, they are labelled, they bear names. As a result, we know the identities of four people who had worked at the facility, three of them medics, one a support person of some description. Identification of one additional medic, closely involved in the clinic's activities, has proven less straightforward. Does the term 'S4' mean anything to either of you, as an identifier?'

'I can honestly say it does not,' said Guerline; Fil shook her head.

Prabha was apparently preparing to ask a further question when a small low-flying object, all bath-bomb fizz and bounce, barrelled into the room and climbed onto her mother's lap. The girl's grandmother appeared shortly thereafter, wearing a vaguely apologetic air. 'Sorry for the intrusion,' said Hara. 'The park just reopened yesterday, after the unpleasantness, and I was going to take Lassa. Would our guests be interested in seeing the meerkats?'

'Me'kat! Me'kat!' said the girl, who'd climbed down from Prabha's chair and was now standing on tiptoes, flicking her face left, right, then left again and laughing.

Prabha checked the guests' expressions before answering. 'That sounds like a wonderful suggestion.' She stood; the others followed suit.

'Actually,' said Prabha, turning to Guerline, 'do you have a moment?' She turned to Hara. 'You go ahead, we'll catch up soon.'

SIXTEEN

With the door shut, Prabha took her seat again. 'I get the feeling you are not telling me everything.'

Guerline sat, busied herself, for rather longer than required, with the task of settling. 'I've been accused in the past,' she began, 'and you yourself have been one of those who've accused it, of sometimes taking things too far. It's a mistake I'm trying not to repeat. Can we leave it at that?'

'Let me speak plainly,' said Prabha. 'It's not ess-four on those labels, though it seems my colleagues still lean in that direction. It's fifty-four, and I know full well who that is signifying, and I think you do too.'

'I would prefer not to answer that.'

'I could compel you to do so,' said Prabha. 'I'm disinclined, but I would prefer to hear your reasons for why this family should be protected.'

Guerline gave her reasons. Braun was silent for several seconds, and then asked, 'How is Hinewai?'

The non sequitur surprised Scarfe, muddled her answer. 'She's… she's a part of my husband's family, my ex-husband's family, not mine. I don't see her much. But she was doing okay, last I saw her.'

'I should be grateful, to her and to you. I would likely have made a different decision, otherwise. And how is your son?'

It took longer than it should have, for Guerline to follow what Prabha Braun was saying. 'I am so sorry for the way it happened,' she said after too long a pause.

'What's past is past,' said Braun. 'And it's far from the worst outcome. Most days she's a delight.'

'My son—Nik—is fine,' said Guerline. 'He wants to take up kiting.'

'Kiting?'

Scarfe told her about the battle-kite club, and the lock licence. 'I'm not sure I'm ready for it.'

'I have something which might help,' said Braun. 'Wait one.' She stood up and left the room. When she returned, she was carrying a weathered flat polymer case, half a metre on its long side, and surprisingly heavy when she handed it to Scarfe.

'What is it?'

'I was Hunten region junior champion, two years in a row. Aged nine and ten. Your son's—Nik's older than that, yes? This is a Xu Stormchaser, an older model by today's standards of course, but they still handle quite well from what I've heard. He'll be fine.'

Guerline sensed herself choke up. 'Thank you,' she said. 'But I couldn't possibly.'

'I've no further use for it,' said Prabha. 'It may as well serve its intended purpose. Though I may end up claiming it back, in seven or eight years, if Lassa shows any interest.'

'Of course,' said Scarfe, not daring to say anything more on the subject.

'We'd best be getting to those meerkats,' said Braun, ushering her guest toward the door.

'Are we done?' Guerline asked.

'I think so,' said Braun, stopping at the door panel. 'We may still call Bayley—Fil's grandfather, that is—to give testimony, but that would likely be only as a witness. What happened wasn't murder, in the sense that the clear intent seems to have been to save lives, rather than destroy them; he didn't abet or have involvement in any deaths. They cut corners, they gave false hope to the terminally ill, but based on the information available to them at the time, the approach should've worked. We'll want to get what further detail we can from Bayley, for an inquest; that'll likely be restricted, in his case, to the falsification of the maps, for which any culpability would long have run out under the statute of limitations. That's not the case for the other, of course, but I agree with you—I think it would be more cruel than productive to pursue that.'

'They were trying to do the right thing,' said Scarfe. 'They thought they *were* doing the right thing.'

'Yes,' said Braun. 'That's always the hell of it, isn't it?'

SEVENTEEN

Scarfe was slow to realise that the walk to the meerkat colony, in Hunten Park's far corner, was for Fil a pilgrimage to Aldous Fischetti's place of death. She found Fil, in the park, standing somewhat away from the others, with a troubled expression on her face. Guerline approached her. 'Are you alright?' she asked.

'Not really,' said Fil, speaking so quietly it was difficult to hear. 'That stuff back there, at Braun's—Grandpa knew all about what had happened to the boy, and the others? I mean, it sounds like there were others. And my mother had some sense of it too, because of how she reacted to the vial.' Fil looked up, turned to Scarfe. 'Did Grandma know?'

'I'm limited in what I can say at the moment. You deserve a full account of this, but… let's say it's under embargo at the moment, while the police investigation continues. There are processes which will need to be gone through. You can call me about it in six months' time, and I can answer all your questions, or you can ask your mother and grandfather about it then. But in the meantime: be there for your grandmother. That's the best advice I can offer you.'

'I don't like being wrapped in cotton wool,' said Bayley.

'Believe me, you're not,' said Scarfe. 'This is something else entirely.'

EIGHTEEN

They arranged railpod freight back to Trafton, for the skidbike and for the kite which Prabha Braun had given Guerline.

Scarfe offered to introduce Fil to Kalinda, in case she opted to move back for the work opportunities available in a larger settlement, but the suggestion was met with no interest. 'I'd just rather get home,' said Fil.

They flew home, two flights as before, but travelling now through the half-hearted darkness of a quiet Xanadu night. This time the layover in Woltjer was just long enough that Guerline paid a quick call to her mother, before it was time to hasten back to the air terminal. Boarding was well underway.

The shipment arrived two days later. 'Open it,' Guerline told him.

Nik removed the casings with sufficient care as to suggest he already knew more or less the contents' nature. His eyes lit up nonetheless.

'It's an old model,' said Guerline. 'A Xu Stormchaser. But I'm told it handles well.'

'Does this mean the lock licence is a yes?'

'Your birthday's next month. I think that will be soon enough.'

'But—'

'And in the meantime, there are sims you can take, so you're familiar with its handling when you do get to try it out.'

'I guess.' Nik didn't look fully convinced. Three weeks was always such a long time at that age.

Scarfe returned to her office, checked her systems. There was a lot to catch up on: the early-onset dementia patient's family, the phloo addiction case, and a couple of new contacts whom Toan had helpfully pointed in her direction. She checked the synopses on the new contacts, made a few preliminary notes on her slate. It'd be good, actually, to be able to immerse herself in some less complicated, or at least less fraught, situations.

She might even aspire to making a habit of it.

EPILOGUE

The slate chirped. Prabha turned over, blearily reached across, checked the display. Adewale. She raised the lights a few percent, gestured the slate's volume down, and signalled *Connect.*

'You at home?'

'Yes,' said Prabha, wondering just where else Kordell Adewale thought she would be at this hour.

'Private, please,' said Adewale.

'Wait one,' said Prabha. She got out of bed, closed the door so her voice wouldn't wake Lassa, spooled out the earbud. Set the slate on its stand on her bedside unit, signalled *View.* 'Okay, proceed.'

Adewale's visage swam into view. Digitally beside it, though likely the women were in two separate other locations, were the faces of Jamali Sabatier and Ryba Ngata.

I should've smartened up for this, Prabha thought ruefully, though her callers showed no indication of any judgment at her appearance.

'We've found something,' said Adewale. 'On Fischetti's slate, which Whiteneck retrieved from the basement earlier today. I've been decanting and analysing its contents since then. I ran a search on 'athermolidizine'. Lots of hits. Most of them are technical as you'd expect, dosage guidelines et cetera, but the item of interest is a personal message, to Sigbjorn Fischetti from Angevin Pechère, advising him in extremely blunt terms to not attempt therapeutic application of the compound.'

'Who is this… Angevin Pechère, and what do you mean by 'extremely blunt terms'?'

'Lead author on two of the three primary studies which originally supported the stuff's use as a cryoprotectant. Based in Melbourne, South Earth somewhere. Dead now, so we can't seek follow-up. Though I suppose we might be able to see if any of the junior authors are still around, and have knowledge of the advice to Fischetti.'

'Extremely blunt terms,' Prabha reminded her, rubbing some sleep from her eye.

'Sorry. The phrase 'invariably fatal' appears in the second sentence, for starters. Repeated a couple more times, if not in so many words. And this is dated a few weeks before the initial publication of the retraction. So presumably when it was in-press, if not before.'

'Can we be sure Fischetti read this message?'

'There's a reply, several days later. I would say it's not particularly direct as a response, it doesn't touch on the lethality aspect at all, but it's pretty clear that he'd read it. He knew the whole time the clinic was in operation.'

'Then why'd he do it?'

'Who knows? He may well have already known he was dying; maybe he hoped the new information was wrong.'

Prabha was silent for several seconds, processing. 'Someone in Melbourne knew what Sigbjorn Fischetti was up to, or what he was planning, at least. Maybe they all did. It sounds, at least, that this wasn't just his secret.'

'Possibly,' said Sabatier. 'But there's a more pressing concern for us. We need to interview Liv Petrakis.'

'Do we have any idea whether she was aware of the message?'

'No idea,' said Adewale. 'This was addressed only to Sigbjorn Fischetti, but he could well have communicated its contents, or it could have been circulated to the others. Their devices are all wiped clean; at least we haven't found anything of theirs that isn't. I suppose when Sigbjorn died, none of them knew how to log in to his.'

'I don't entirely like the idea of interviewing Petrakis, at her age and in her condition,' said Prabha. 'But I can see it's needful. Would we send a team to Trafton, rather than bringing her here?'

'Yes,' said Sabatier. 'We'll liaise with Trafton pol. I'll emphasise to them that this will need a sensitive and intelligent approach. That has governed my choice of team members too. Ryba here will go; I want you to accompany her.'

'Me? But I'm not that long back from a week in the field,' Prabha complained. 'Lassa is going to forget what I look like.'

'It can't be helped,' said Sabatier. 'I envisage just a short visit, a day, maybe two, unless matters complicate themselves. It's highly likely we wouldn't seek to bring charges, even if she had a level of foreknowledge which would technically amount to homicide, in the boy's case at least. As you've noted, she's far enough gone that she likely wouldn't live long enough for sentencing.'

'Then why even question her?'

'To get to the truth,' said Ryba Ngata. 'It's possible this might even bring a sort of absolution for her, over something she's been living with, concealing, her whole adult life. With it dealt with, she can perhaps move on. Or let go.'

To a higher plane of existence. Yeah, right, Prabha thought to herself. She held her tongue.

'It would be a good idea,' Sabatier added, meeting Prabha's gaze through the screen, 'if you can also brief that Trafton caseworker, the one who was here last week with the granddaughter. That family's going to need some support.'

ACKNOWLEDGMENTS

Hearty thanks once again to James Morrison, who has double duty on this book, in the context of editing and cover illustration. For the latter, James's artwork incorporates elements of images by iStock/Stefana Popa (hand) and iStock/Mariusz Prusaczyk (ice texture).

Any residual errors in this text are, of course, my own work.

ABOUT THE AUTHOR

Born and raised in North Canterbury, New Zealand, Simon Petrie now lives in Canberra, Australia, where he is paid to be careful with words. He has been shortlisted several times for the Sir Julius Vogel, Ditmar, and Aurealis Awards, and has won the Sir Julius Vogel Award three times: in 2010 for Best New Talent and in 2013 and 2018, with *Flight 404* and *Matters Arising from the Identification of the Body* respectively, for Best Novella. He also scored a coveted Dishonourable Mention in the 2011 Bulwer-Lytton Fiction Contest.

He has edited five issues (numbers 35, 40, 51, 54, and 61) of *Andromeda Spaceways Inflight Magazine*, and has co-edited two anthologies (*Light Touch Paper, Stand Clear* and *Use Only As Directed*) with Edwina Harvey and one (*Next*) with Rob Porteous.

A former researcher in both laboratory and computational chemistry, Simon's publishing history also includes numerous studies on the upper-atmosphere chemistry of Titan; on the ion/molecule chemistry of the dense interstellar cloud TMC-1 and the circumstellar envelope of the post-asymptotic-giant-branch star IRC+10216; on the gas-phase chemistry of multiply-charged fullerene ions; and on the structure of the active site of the water-oxidising complex within Photosystem II. He holds actionable views in support of second person present tense, em-dashes, and Oxford commas.

BOOKS BY SIMON PETRIE

THE GUERLINE SCARFE MYSTERIES

Matters Arising from the Identification of the Body
Guerline Scarfe, a caseworker in a midsized urban habitat on Titan, investigates the events surrounding the death of Tanja Morgenstein.
(Winner of the 2018 Sir Julius Vogel award for Best Novella.)
Paperback: 978-0-6483228-0-1
Ebook: 978-0-6483228-1-8

Reappraisal of the Circumstances Resulting in Death
While Guerline Scarfe looks for answers in the disappearance of materials science researcher Alejandro Driscoll, a junior pol officer probes the discovery of human remains at a mining installation within Titan's Afekan Crater.
Paperback: 978-0-6483837-0-3

Consideration of the Method of Disposal
A single-vehicle skidbike accident, amid Titan's icy wastes, leaves geochem worker Fil Bayley traumatised. Guerline Scarfe, working to understand the trauma's source, uncovers a chilling, long-hidden secret.
Paperback: 978-0-6483837-1-0

Flight 404

The search for the *Bougainvillaea* brings investigator Charmaine Mertz back to the unwelcoming world of her boyhood.
(Winner of the 2013 Sir Julius Vogel award for Best Novella.)
Paperback: 978-0-6483228-4-9
Ebook: 978-0-6483228-5-6

Tremendously Inconveniencing A Great Many Photons

An uplifting First Contact novel, as the stupidly large spaceship *List of Wealthy Donors*, populated by experts of every type, journeys through hyperspace towards the source of a mysterious radio signal emanating from the Galaxy's inner reaches.
Paperback: 978-0-6483836-1-1
Ebook: 978-0-6483836-2-8

Wayfaring Stranger

Aboard the research airship *Wayfaring Stranger*, newcomer Solveig Robertson struggles to find a place alongside her colleagues, while the airborne creatures Solveig is most keen to study—the gargantual and sentient zeps—show no interest in human contact.
Paperback: 978-0-6483836-7-3

SHORT FICTION COLLECTIONS

Murder On The Zenith Express (the Gordon Mamon collection)
Lift operator and reluctant detective Gordon Mamon contends with the
many deaths which seem unfairly to keep happening in his space-elevator
hotel module.
Paperback: 978-0-6483228-8-7
Ebook: 978-0-6483228-9-4

80,000 Totally Secure Passwords That No Hacker Would Ever Guess
A motley of whimsy, SF, and stories improved by dinosaurs.
Paperback: 978-0-6483228-6-3
Ebook: 978-0-6483228-7-0

The 1001 Top Immortality Treatments You Must Try Before You Die
Another motley, including also a stray Titan story and possibly the last
Gordon Mamon mystery story.
Paperback: 978-0-6483836-3-5
Ebook: 978-0-6483836-4-2

I Have No Legs And I Must Manspread
A shorter collection than the previous two, but if anything more motley
than either of those. If you only ever read one piece of fiction by me,
make it 'Of Why The Sea', in this one.
Paperback: 978-0-6483836-8-0